"We Alexanders do not get divorces."

Rans eyed her mockingly as she spoke. "And so they live miserably ever after. An Alexander makes a wrong decision and lives with it the rest of his life, without a second chance, a martyr to tradition."

"I'm not interested in a second chance. Once is enough for me," Lara declared loftily.

"So you hold yourself aloof from the animal desires that plague the rest of mankind. What a waste of such womanly beauty," he said, reaching out to touch her cheek.

"Don't touch me!" she snapped, pushing his hand away as if his fingertips had burned her skin.

"You're afraid you might like it?"

"Never!" Lara hissed.

The sun lines at the corners of his eyes crinkled at her defiant challenge. "Never?" he murmured huskily.

JANET DAILEY AMERICANA

A TRADITION OF PRIDE

Harlequin Books

TORONTO • NEW YORK • LONDON
AMSTERDAM • PARIS • SYDNEY • HAMBURG
STOCKHOLM • ATHENS • TOKYO • MILAN
MADRID • WARSAW • BUDAPEST • AUCKLAND

The state flower depicted on the cover of this book is
magnolia.

Janet Dailey Americana edition published May 1987
Second printing June 1988
Third printing June 1989
Fourth printing July 1990
Fifth printing September 1991
Sixth printing January 1992

ISBN 0-373-89874-6

Harlequin Presents edition published April 1981

Original hardcover edition published in 1980
by Mills & Boon Limited

A TRADITION OF PRIDE

Printed in U.S.A.

CHAPTER ONE

RANS MACQUADE PAUSED on the porch of the brick cottage. Overhead, the morning sun was bright in a cloudless sky. A cool northwest breeze rustled through the pines, carrying a chilling January nip to the air. He allowed his corded jacket of wheat tan to swing open, indifferent to the temperature.

The sweep of his narrowed brown eyes encountered the long, straight rows of pecan trees in the rolling field across the road from the cottage. They were wooden skeletons without their summer foliage, stretching in seemingly endless lines.

The firm line of his mouth curved upward at the corners in satisfaction, carving masculine dimples in his lean cheeks. All of this was virtually his. He was in complete charge with a free hand over the entire operation of Alexander land.

Nothing less would have induced him to leave Texas to move to southern Mississippi. Rans Mac-Quade had made that clear to Martin Alexander before he accepted the position. The man had given his word that Rans would be in total control and Rans welcomed the challenge of it. After nearly two full months, Rans was willing to concede that Martin Alexander was a man of his word.

A quick glance at his watch reminded him of the time. Smooth, effortless strides carried him down the steps to the pickup truck parked next to the cottage. The breeze rumpled the wayward thickness of his tobacco-brown hair. His fingers raked it carelessly into a semblance of order as he climbed into the cab of the forest-green and white truck.

It was only a short drive to the main house. Normally Rans would have walked through the stand of pines between his cottage and the Alexander home, but after going over last year's production report in detail with Martin Alexander, he was driving to the cattle barns. It was more practical to leave from the main house.

The Alexander home was an imposing structure, although not the typically palatial Southern plantation. The Spanish influence was evident in its austere design and the liberal usage of lacy grillwork. The grandness of age was understated. Many times Rans had seen it in the early evening hours, the windows ablaze with welcoming light. It was first a home and second a house.

At the front door, Rans let the brass knocker fall three times. He was not yet that familiar with his employer to walk into his home unannounced. So he waited, a thumb hooked in his belt loop while he absently studied the white enameled door and the flanking windows that ran the length of it, protected by intricate iron scrollwork.

The door opened and his gaze shifted to meet a pair of jet dark eyes on the same level with his own. Considering Rans's height of six foot one, it was not an occurrence that happened often.

"Good morning, MacQuade." There was a flash of white teeth as the man smiled and opened the door wider. "You must be here to see Martin. Come on in."

"Good morning, Trevor." Rans returned the greeting diffidently as he stepped into the entrance hall. "Martin's expecting me."

"Yes, I know." Trevor Cochran smiled again. "He's on a long-distance telephone call right now. Why don't you go into the living room and make yourself comfortable? He shouldn't be long. Would you like some coffee, tea or anything while you're waiting?"

"No." A brief negative shake accompanied his reply.

"I'll let Martin know you're here." With a condescending nod, the tall, dark-haired man moved off in the direction of the study.

Rans's gaze lingered on the man's back before he turned toward the open double doors to the living room. A muscle twitched briefly along his hard jaw and he recognized the cause of his impatience to be Trevor Cochran.

When Rans had arrived the last of November to take charge, he had been surprised and curious to discover that Martin Alexander had a young and intelligent son-in-law, Trevor Cochran. He was the husband of Martin's only child, the heir apparent of the vast Alexander holdings. Presumably Martin should have been grooming his son-in-law to take over the reins. Instead he had offered Rans a long-term contract giving him total charge of the farm.

Mentally Rans had braced himself for the hostility he had expected Martin's decision to bring. Yet Trevor Cochran hadn't seemed at all perturbed by the turn of events. Although Trevor had an active role in the company and lived with his wife in the same house with his father-in-law, he seemed satisfied that someone else was solely responsible for the operation.

Even while he recognized Trevor's lack of ambition, Rans couldn't understand it. He didn't know how anyone could be a part of an operation this size and not rush out to aggressively meet the challenge of running it smoothly and successfully.

There was another factor to be recognized, too. Despite Trevor Cochran's muscular physique, he was physically soft. He was neither able nor willing to meet the physical demands of the position. His prowess, Rans decided, was limited to the bedroom. With Trevor's dark, rather stunning good looks, it had probably been put to considerable use—and still was, if the rumors were accurate.

Pushing the draperies of green brocade aside, Rans gazed out the window at the expanse of well-kept lawn shaded by towering pines. Footsteps sounded on the tiled floor of the hallway, followed by a second, lighter pair. He released the draperies and turned expectantly.

"Sara." It was Trevor Cochran's voice, and Rans sighed impatiently at the delay in meeting with Martin Alexander. "Has my wife been down this morning? She wasn't at the breakfast table."

"Lara—Mrs. Cochran," the housekeeper corrected herself quickly, "had breakfast in her room about an hour ago."

"In her room." An eyebrow arched swiftly as Rans smiled with cynical amusement. He thought separate bedrooms had gone out with hooped skirts. However, it did explain the first gossip he had heard on his arrival—that Trevor Cochran spent more time with other women than he did with his wife.

"But she hasn't been down?" Trevor Cochran repeated from the hall. "Are you sure?"

"Were you looking for me, Trevor?" A second female voice drifted into the living room from the large hall. It was firm, very cool and composed, yet soft and faintly husky.

A fiery color caught Rans's eye. Instantly his gaze focused on the large, ornate mirror in the living room. From his angle it reflected the scene in the hallway, showing the lower half of the staircase where Lara Alexander Cochran had paused.

She was strikingly beautiful. There was no other way to describe her. As Rans openly studied her reflection in the mirror, he felt the stirring of his pulse. She was wearing a tweed suit of ocher gold and brown, while revealing a shapely pair of legs. Despite its bulkiness, the material of her suit seemed to cling to the curve of her thighs and hips. The molding lines of the jacket suggested the slenderness of her waist and the jutting firmness of her breasts, which Rans knew would fill the cupping of his large hands.

If her disturbingly shapely female figure didn't attract a man's attention, then Rans knew the striking combination of shimmering red gold hair and green eyes would. To top it off, Lara Cochran had a face to complement everything else—a vision of perfection from the delicate wing of her brow down a classically straight nose to a mouth with a sensually full lower lip.

The housekeeper discreetly left the couple alone in the hallway, but Rans felt no such compunction to halt his hidden observation.

"Yes, I was looking for you," Trevor replied to her question. "I knocked at your door, but you didn't answer."

"Knocked at your door." Again his mouth twitched in dry amusement. This marriage was taking on the overtones of a Victorian novel.

"I was probably taking a bath and didn't hear

you." Lara shrugged eloquently and descended the last few steps. "I was just on my way out. What did you want?"

Her marble features were completely devoid of expression as she tilted her head upward to gaze at her husband's face. Rans's eyes narrowed on her reflection.

The key word was "marble." The smooth, classic beauty of her face seemed to be carved out of that hard, white stone, with any imperfection polished away, leaving a hard veneer devoid of any animation. It was probably the reason Rans appreciated her loveliness without feeling a surge of lust in his loins. She was a cold work of art.

"I arranged my schedule at the office so that I could take today off," Trevor was saying, the handsome mouth curving into a winning smile guaranteed to set a female heart fluttering. Yet Lara Cochran seemed unmoved by its decided charm. "It's been so long since we've had a day to ourselves that I thought we might drive to the gulf coast."

Glistening copper-colored lips curved into a smile of insincere apology. "I'm on my way to Lumberton, Trevor."

"What's in Lumberton?" His smooth forehead was faintly drawn into a frown.

"Angie Connors," was the composed response. "Her husband flew down to Longleaf to do some quail hunting and she came along."

"Angie Connors," he thoughtfully repeated

the name. "She's the brunette who was matron of honor at our wedding, wasn't she? The two of you went to college together."

"That's right." Lara Cochran turned away as she answered. By her actions, Rans MacQuade guessed that she was looking at herself in the oval hall mirror. "It's been over two years since we've had a chance to get together, and she'll be leaving the day after tomorrow."

Rans watched the long, slender fingers smooth the liquid-fire hair away from her face, although he could not remember ever seeing a strand out of place. And always she wore it pulled back in a coil or a bun to emphasize the classic beauty of her features. He had never seen it falling loose around her shoulders where the breeze could play with it or a man could run his fingers through the red gold tresses.

"I never did have a chance to get to know her. I'll come along with you." Trevor stated. "It's only right that I become better acquainted with your best friend."

"No." The refusal was instant yet smoothly firm. "You would only be bored, Trevor. Besides, I'm sure daddy would much prefer that you are at the office today, regardless of whether you can arrange to be away or not."

Trevor's expression darkened. "Lara—" He seemed about to argue the point when a hallway door opened and closed out of range of Rans's limited view.

"Trevor, did you say Rans had arrived?"

At the sound of Martin Alexander's voice, Rans glanced away from the mirror, letting his gaze focus indifferently on the blackened hearth of the fireplace.

"He's in the living room. I'll get him," Trevor replied tightly.

"Good morning, dad." Lara Cochran's warm greeting to her father echoed above Trevor's quiet summons as he paused in the open doorway of the living room. Rans took his time moving toward the hall, lighting a cigarette as he walked.

"Good morning, pet." Martin Alexander returned his daughter's greeting with definite affection. "I missed you at breakfast this morning."

"I indulged myself and had it in bed." The laughing words were uttered as Rans stepped into the hall. Yet her green eyes were aloof when they swung to him. "Good morning, Mr. MacQuade."

"Mrs. Cochran." Briefly he inclined his head to acknowledge her greeting before turning to his employer. "Hello, Martin."

"Since you two are obviously running off to closet yourselves in the study and talk business—" Lara removed a set of car keys from her brown purse "—I might as well make my exit now. I've already told Sara I won't be home for lunch."

"Take care," her father smiled. "And give Angie my hello."

"I'll walk you to the car darling." Trevor slipped his hand under her elbow.

With almost practiced ease, she slipped free of his touch. "That isn't necessary," Lara answered coolly. "We can say our goodbyes here."

Through the smoke from his cigarette, Rans noted the tightening of Trevor's jaw. As if aware of his audience, Trevor smiled automatically and graciously accepted her wish.

"Very well." His dark head bent to kiss her. At the very last second, Lara moved her head slightly so that his mouth brushed the smoothness of her cheek instead of her lips.

"I'll see you at dinner." She smiled at her husband without warmth or emotion and moved to the front door with unaffected grace.

One corner of Rans's mouth lifted sardonically as he turned to follow Martin to the study. His sympathy was directed to Trevor. He had married a cold witch with red hair. Why was it, Rans wondered idly to himself, that the truly beautiful women always seemed to be frigid? And poor Martin, imagine having that hollow shell of a woman as a daughter. Perhaps being her father blinded him to all but her exquisite loveliness.

LARA WAS TEN MILES south of the farm and Hattiesburg before the inner tension began to ease and she could relax. The highway was a tree-lined avenue of pines. The peaceful scenery released her mind from its self-imprisonment and let it wander.

Sunlight flashed on the diamond solitaire of her wedding ring. A small sigh of relief escaped her lips that Trevor had been unable to force his company on her today—not that he often tried anymore.

Her fingers tightened around the steering wheel as she remembered Trevor's announcement that he was free to spend the day with her, as if she was supposed to be so grateful that she should have fallen to her knees. If the prospect wasn't so revolting, it would have been laughable.

The thought brought back the image of the cynical look that had been in Ransom MacQuade's eyes. Lara knew what he had been thinking—that she was a cold, unfeeling bitch, pampered and spoiled by her father. Men always stick together.

A shiver of apprehension danced down her spine—the same sensation she had experienced the first time she had met him. Her father had brought him to dinner one evening a day or two after Ransom MacQuade had taken over the management of Alexander land.

Compared to her husband, Ransom MacQuade was not a handsome man. His features were too boldly chiseled. Yet his virility and vitality made him compellingly attractive, forces equally as potent as Trevor's considerable charm and looks.

His hair was not jet black like Trevor's, but in varying shades of brown, like tobacco. His eyes were the same brown, seemingly lazy in their regard yet never missing anything. Although the same height as Trevor, Ransom MacQuade was the larger of the two. Lara had seen the rippling of his muscles beneath his shirt and knew there wasn't an ounce of spare flesh on him.

After nearly two months, she still hadn't decided what there was about him that she didn't trust, that made her feel so apprehensive whenever he was around. Maybe it was simply because he was a man.

Her father certainly thought highly of him, although her father tended to think highly of most people. He was a born optimist. Not that Lara questioned Ransom MacQuade's credentials. When her father had requested her opinion of him after their first meeting, she hadn't cast any doubts on his ability nor did she endorse her father's choice.

"I think his decisiveness borders on arrogance," she had replied.

It had drawn a chauvinistic laugh from her father. Then he had expounded on MacQuade's qualifications, his extensive breeding experience with Santa Gertrudis cattle, the mainstay of the Alexander farm, coupled with an excellent knowledge of pecan orchards. So in the face of her father's hearty approval, Lara had not voiced any more intuitive comments that warned her against Ransom MacQuade.

The car slowed. Lara glanced around her in surprise. She was on a county road that turned into the lane leading to Longleaf Plantation. She had been so lost in thought she hadn't even been aware of where she was. One part of her mind must have been, since she had made all the right turns to get here. With a shake of her head, she tried to banish all the unwanted thoughts and concentrate on seeing Angie again.

Tall pine trees towered over the landscape to shade the vast lawn. The evergreens were of the longleaf variety that had given the private hunting lodge its name. The sun glistened on the mirror-smooth surface of a small lake. A graveled driveway curved lazily through the sylvan setting, ending at the rustic elegance of the rough-hewn cypress buildings of Longleaf.

A full smile spread across Lara's face at the sight of the petite brunette leaning against the porch railing, dressed in a bulky blue sweater that looked several sizes too large and slim-fitting wool slacks. At the honk of the car's horn, Angie Connors raced down the steps, waving excitedly and reaching the car as it stopped in front of the main lodge.

Lara was barely out of the car when she was wrapped in an exuberant hug. "Just look at you!" Angie exclaimed, her dark eyes dancing with happiness. "My, but don't you look like a lady!"

Laughing, Lara shook away the comment. A tight lump entered her throat as she gazed at her best friend whom she hadn't seen in so long. On the surface, Angie hadn't changed. There was still a mass of dark, waving curls on her head, styled to show off her petite femininity and add a spice of impish mischief.

"You haven't changed a bit," Lara sighed, but she couldn't stop herself from wondering if, like herself, Angie had changed on the inside.

"In two years was I supposed to grow fangs?" she teased, then bit into her lower lip. "It's so good to see you again," Angie added in a choked voice filled with emotion. "This is so much better than a thousand letters. We have so much to catch up on. Tell me about Trevor. How is he?"

Lara turned away, reaching into the car to get her purse. "He's fine," she answered noncommittally.

"Is he still the handsome devil who whisked you off on your honeymoon before the wedding reception had barely begun?" Angie laughed.

"The same." But Lara's answering laugh was decidedly brittle. "And Bob, how's he?"

A puzzled light fleetingly entered Angie's dark eyes before she was sidetracked by Lara's question. "The mighty hunter is fine. The hunting party should be back any time and you can see for yourself. It's nearly lunchtime and Bob has an alarm clock in his tummy that goes off at breakfast, lunch and dinner time." As if on cue, the first of the hunting jeeps rumbled into sight. "See what I mean?" Angie laughed as she spied her husband in the front seat with the guide.

The straggling arrival of the various hunting parties from different areas of the plantation kept the excitement of the morning's quail hunt running until lunchtime. Angie and Lara, the only two women, were natural choices for the dozen hunters to relate their adventures.

Through lunch, the two friends had exchanged only surface comments about their lives. The conversation was dominated by the men, not that Lara objected. She kept seeing that radiant glow that filled Angie's expression every time she looked at her husband. It twisted her heart with a bitter sadness.

Sitting on the black leather sofa in the main lounge, Lara gazed sightlessly into the flames licking at the logs in the massive fireplace. Her pensive mood separated her from the hunters preparing to leave for the afternoon shoot. Absently she flicked the ash from her cigarette into the ashtray.

It was a cozy yet spacious room. The unfinished cypress wood in the open-beamed ceiling also paneled the walls. The large, small-paned windows let the outdoors come in. But Lara was unaware of the natural charm of the room.

"Well, Lara, are you going to tell me what happened?"

Angie's voice caught her off guard. She glanced up in surprise. The room was empty. The hunters gone. There were only the two of them and Angie was leaning forward in a large cushioned chair, her expressive face calm and serious.

Snubbing the cigarette out in the ashtray, Lara shook her head. "I don't know what you're talking about," she smiled and tried to look blank.

"Yes, you do," her friend answered patiently. "And I want to know what's happened to change you."

"I haven't changed," Lara protested. There was suddenly nothing for her nervous hands to do and she reached again for the cigarette pack sitting on the table.

"Of course not," Angie agreed with tongue in cheek. "Which is why the Lara, who two years ago could hardly be persuaded to have a cigarette at a bar, is now chain-smoking."

"Smoking isn't a crime—a health hazard, but not a crime." She set the pack down, avoiding her friend's gaze.

"And you've become defensive. The openness I remember is gone. Each time I ask anything that remotely resembles a personal question, you withdraw. There isn't any other way to describe it. Oh, you answer me," Angie laughed abruptly without humor, "but it's always a standard response that tells nothing. I've done all the talking with my Bob this and Bob that. You've barely mentioned Trevor's name. What's wrong?"

Lara stared at her twisting fingers. "It's the classic syndrome in every marriage." Her voice was hard and deliberately uncaring. "Didn't you recognize it? It's commonly known as 'the honeymoon is over.'"

"Nothing is as simple as that." The dark curls bounced in a definite negative shake. "At your wedding, you were happier than I had ever seen you. Something has to have happened to make that change."

Her fingers wearily rubbed her forehead. A pain had begun to throb in her temples. "Maybe I was happy then. I don't remember anymore," Lara sighed. "I was a stupid, blind little bride, lost in a fantasy world of romance complete with a tall, dark and handsome Prince Charming."

"Trevor...." Angie hesitated. "Doesn't he love you?"

"Of course." Lara's mouth twisted into a wry smile. "I'm Lara Alexander. He also loves Julie, Ann, Connie—speak a girl's name and he loves her. But I'm Lara Alexander so he married me."

"Are you sure? I mean, about the other women?"

"Oh, yes." She took a deep breath, pressing her lips tightly together. She hadn't expected to feel pain about that again, but it wasn't really pain. It was pride. "I am very sure about the other women."

A hand closed over the clasped fingers in Lara's lap. Her green eyes met the look of commiseration glistening in Angie's dark eyes. But Lara's own expression remained blank from long practice.

"How did you find out?" Angie whispered.

"Not quite three months after the wedding, Trevor called the house one afternoon to tell me he was going to be working late on some reports daddy wanted. Me, in my rose-colored glasses and with grains of rice still in my hair, decided to surprise him. I packed a dinner and wrapped a bottle of champagne in a cooler and went tripping along to the office. I expected to find him poring over papers on his desk. Instead he was on the couch with his blond secretary."

"Lara, I'm sorry." The offer of sympathy was issued tautly. "What did he say? Did he explain?"

"There wasn't a great deal to explain, was there?" Lara countered dryly. "I left the office immediately and Trevor came rushing home full of explanations. We had an enormous fight. I went around for days silently weeping and wailing and beating my chest trying to figure out what *I* had done wrong. Then I became filled with bitterness and revenge and flirted outrageously with any man I met, trying to pay Trevor back and make him jealous."

"Didn't he promise to stop?" Angie frowned.

Lara nodded mutely. "And for a while I believed him." Her impassive green eyes slid to the tortured expression on her friend's face. "You would be surprised at the depths you sink to when you stop trusting your husband. I went through his personal papers and found rent receipts for an apartment in Hattiesburg. It was his private little love nest. I couldn't be sure he still used it after his promise, so I followed him one day when he made a trip into town, ostensibly to meet an attorney friend. The meeting turned out to be an assignation and the attorney had a striking resemblance to the blond secretary Trevor had supposedly discharged." Without conscious thought, she lighted another cigarette and inhaled the smoke deeply. "For all I know the apartment is still in use, although I believe the girl has changed several times. Trevor is always discreet. He has to maintain his respectable standing in the community."

"How did your father react to this? I can't imagine him tolerating this treatment of you." It was Angie's turn to clasp her hands together.

"Angie—" Lara laughed hollowly "—my father is a Victorian chauvinist. One of the first things I did when I learned Trevor was cheating on me was to run to daddy and cry out my woes. His words of comfort consisted of a lengthy explanation that just because a man steps out on his wife doesn't mean he no longer loves her. I had the impression that, as a lady, I was supposed to be grateful that Trevor didn't expect me to endure all of his manly passion."

"You're kidding?" Angie stared at her in openmouthed disbelief. "Thank heavens Bob doesn't feel that way." She leaned back in her chair. "Surely when your father saw what it was doing to you, he had more to suggest than grin and bear it."

"His antiquated notion was the old standby that I should have a child." Lara rose to her feet, walked aimlessly to the sliding glass windows and stared through the small panes. "I couldn't bring myself to tell him that Trevor and I hadn't slept together since I had found him with his secretary and the thought of any intimacy with him made me ill."

A stillness permeated the room. The fire crackled in the hearth while outside the laughing babble could be heard as the waters of Black Creek rushed over the curve of rocks. A rocking chair on the porch overlooking the creek was stirred into movement by the breeze.

"Lara, what are you going to do?" Angie broke the silence at last. "You surely aren't going to maintain this marital farce, are you?"

Lara turned away from the peaceful outdoor scene. None of her composure had been the least bit affected by any of the incidents and emotions she had just related. Time had reinforced her armor to the point that it was nearly impenetrable.

"Do you remember meeting my Aunt Beatrice from Gulfport at the wedding?" Lara inquired. At Angie's bewildered nod, she continued. "The morning of the wedding she took me aside, taking my mother's place and giving me all the advice and instruction a bride needs. One of the things she stressed most fervently was the fact that in all the history of the Alexander family, there had never been a divorce. It's a tradition that everyone is very proud of, including my father. In essence, she said that even if love dies, a couple should stay together regardless of whether or not they destroy each other's souls in the process."

"Family loyalty is one thing, but you are carrying it too far!'' Angie protested vigorously. "You can't ruin your life because of someone else's out-moded beliefs!''

"I agree.'' With one cigarette out, Lara lighted another, exhaling a cloud of smoke and watching it dissipate in the air. "But I don't see any point in getting a divorce. True, I'd be rid of Trevor, but in everything but name, I'm rid of him now. He's just a man living under the same roof that I do. I don't love him anymore, nor do I hate him. I simply don't care about him, period.''

Angie raised her hands in a helplessly beseeching plea for Lara to reconsider what she was saying. "But...you'll meet another man someday and want to marry him and have his children.''

"No.'' Pity flashed in her green eyes, knowing her friend was seeing life through the rose-colored glasses she herself had once worn. "I know I must sound hard and cynical to you, but I don't care to have any man in my life...ever.''

"You can't mean that," Angie sighed. "It's not natural.''

"I've lived the life of a celibate for nearly two years. It's really not so difficult." Lara glanced at her left hand, watching the play of light on her diamond. "This wedding ring insulates me. If it was off, I would be fair game, and I would just as soon not have any men around. So Trevor can have whatever status and money he feels is a part of the Alexander family—and his girl friends— and I'll have the solitary life I want.''

"Do you expect me to believe that you've stopped feeling, Lara?" Angie asked quietly.

"Feeling toward a man the way you mean? Yes, I have stopped feeling. I've tasted the so-called marital bliss, and it was bitterly galling," was her positive reply.

"It won't last," her friend murmured, her dark eyes rounded with deep sadness.

Lara smiled confidently. "We'll see."

CHAPTER TWO

LARA CAREFULLY POURED the brandied syrup over the salad of assorted fruits and nuts in the stemmed serving glasses and set the emptied cup in the sink. A pecan pie was cooling on the counter, the flaky golden crust complementing the toast-brown pecan halves.

"As far as I'm concerned, Sara," she smiled, "you can skip the meal and serve the pie. It looks delicious."

"And fattening," was the reply. "Not that you'll ever have to worry."

"Is there anything else I can help you with?" Lara wiped her hands on a towel and glanced around the kitchen.

The housekeeper paused near the oven door. "You can carry the wineglasses into the dining room. They were covered with waterspots again. You're going to have to talk to your father about that dishwasher. It's next to worthless if I have to keep redoing everything I put in it."

"I will," Lara promised, picking up the wineglasses. "Anything else?"

"No." Sara opened the oven door and peered

inside. "Don't let your father linger over his whiskey. I don't want to overcook this quail."

"All I'll have to do is tell him that you're serving his favorite and he'll probably be at the table before the quail is done." Lara pushed the free-swinging kitchen door open with her elbow, taking care not to knock the crystal glasses in her hand. "I don't know what dad would do if Henry didn't go hunting every couple of weeks."

"Henry didn't bring us the quail," Sara corrected, her words checking Lara's exit from the kitchen. "He's down with arthritis again."

"I didn't know." She tipped her head curiously to the side, the red gold coil atop her head shimmered with fire from the overhead light. "Who did give us the quail?"

"Mr. MacQuade."

"Oh," Lara murmured and pushed on through the doorway. As the door swung back, she wondered idly if Ransom MacQuade had known of her father's taste for quail and brought them to edge up higher in his book. She supposed he had. It never hurt to keep scoring points with the boss.

There was a knock at the door as Lara set the wineglasses around the three place settings at the table. From the kitchen, she heard Sara's grumble and smiled inwardly. "I'll answer it, Sara," she called, touching fingertips to her hair, making sure there were no escaping tendrils.

Her heels clicked loudly on the tiled floor of the hallway. Before Lara reached the front door, there was another knock and she wondered who the impatient visitor could be arriving at the dinner hour. She swung the door open.

The polite smile of greeting froze at the sight of Ransom MacQuade. Her green eyes focused in shock on the bouquet of red roses he held in his hands. Slicing to his face, her gaze searched bewilderedly for an explanation.

"Good evening, Mrs. Cochran." His glittering brown eyes lazily surveyed her from top to bottom. "That's a homey touch," he mocked. "May I come in?"

For an instant, Lara didn't understand his comment until she realized she had not taken off the gingham apron that protected her apricot dress. A hand nervously smoothed the front of it as she swung the door open wider to admit him.

"Of course, Mr. MacQuade. Please come in." Her voice was totally composed, offering no sign that she had been flustered even for a second. "You'll have to forgive my appearance. Dinner is nearly ready to be served."

Her gaze slid briefly across his wide shoulders, noting the flawless cut of the forest-green leisure suit and the cream-colored shirt, opened at the throat.

"My timing is perfect then." The suggestion of dimples appeared in his angular cheeks.

The wing of one eyebrow lifted slightly at his comment. Was he inviting himself to dinner, Lara wondered. Remembering the amount of food that had been prepared, she knew it would be straining even Sara's capabilities to stretch the servings to four people. Rather than tell him he couldn't stay, Lara chose to ignore his comment.

The roses were offered to her. "These are for you, I believe," Rans said dryly.

She hesitated for a split second before reluctantly accepting them. "Thank you, Mr. MacQuade. This is very kind of you, but not necessary." Lara fingered the small card attached to the bouquet. Why on earth was he giving her flowers?

"They aren't from me." Laughter danced behind his hooded look. "A florist delivery man was at the door when I came. He had several other stops to make so he asked me to give them to you."

At the first sensation of warmth touching her cheeks, Lara turned away from his mocking and speculative gaze. The trouble with having red hair was that she tended to blush too easily. It had been ages since she had committed an embarrassing blunder like this. It was a novelty to discover she was still capable of blushing.

Curiosity led her to remove the card from its small envelope. The familiar handwriting satisfied Lara before she even read the message. The words were simple: "For my wife. Happy Valentine's Day, darling. Trevor."

Her mouth twitched cynically at the corners. She had so completely blocked out all the romantic notions from her mind that when she had glanced at the calendar this morning and noticed the date was February fourteenth, it hadn't meant anything to her. Trevor, the inveterate Romeo that he was, would never overlook any romantic occasion.

"From a secret admirer?" Rans's husky voice questioned from behind her.

Lara slipped the card back in its envelope, an indifferently cool smile curving her lips as she turned slightly toward him. Her complexion again was the smooth color of marble.

"A Valentine gift from my husband," she responded. "I hope I didn't embarrass you by thinking the roses were from you."

"Not at all," Rans shrugged, his roving gaze moving over the fiery crown of her coiled hair. "I wouldn't have chosen red roses, anyway. They clash with your hair." His attention shifted to the artistically draped folds that formed the neckline of her dress. "The shade of your dress would have been more suitable."

His observation was so impersonally offered that it was impossible for Lara to take offense at his remark. She had the impression that although Rans MacQuade might find her attractive, he was definitely not interested in her. There was faint arrogance in his dismissal of her as a desirable woman, but Lara experienced only relief at the knowledge.

"But red roses are a symbol of love." Trevor had descended the stairs unseen to pause on the landing before making his presence known. The charcoal-gray suit and matching vest he wore perfectly complemented his dark good looks. He flashed a smile at Lara and traversed the last few steps. "I'm glad they were delivered before I had to leave, darling."

Leave? Lara hadn't been aware that he was going anywhere, but she was disinclined to admit it in front of Rans MacQuade. She touched a delicate red petal.

"The roses are beautiful, Trevor. Thank you." It was spoken without the warmth of sincerity.

Long strides carried Trevor to her side. His hand cupped the flower of the petal she had just touched and his head bent to sniff its fragrance.

"It was the least I could do since the monthly club dinner was scheduled for this evening." He gazed deeply into her cool green eyes. Lara was unmoved by his supposed adoration. If she felt anything, it was amusement that his male ego was still determined to win back her affection. He couldn't seem to stand it when a woman was indifferent to him. "It's my way of saying I'm sorry I can't be with you tonight."

"I understand," Lara nodded.

"I have to leave or I'll be late." Trevor brushed a kiss across her cheek.

"Does Sara know you won't be here for dinner?" Lara inquired as an afterthought.

"I reminded her this morning. I'll probably have a drink with the others when the meeting is over. If I'm late getting home, don't wait up for me," was his parting remark as he moved toward the door.

As if she would, Lara thought. Watching Trevor leave, her gaze accidentally focused on Rans MacQuade's rugged profile, also observing her husband's departure. The knowing gleam in his brown eyes told Lara that he too was guessing that Trevor's drink with the others referred to the female sex and not the male club members. Trevor, she thought cynically, do you really think you are fooling anyone but yourself?

The incident had answered another question that had been forming. The third place setting at the table, Rans MacQuade's unexpected appearance, and Sara's previous knowledge that Trevor wouldn't be dining at home this evening—obviously Rans's offering of the quail had elicited an invitation to dinner.

As if feeling her gaze, Rans turned to meet it. The knowing gleam left the velvet brown of his eyes as they assumed a thoughtfully measuring look, silently trying to judge if Lara had guessed Trevor's evening would end in some other woman's arms. Pride elevated her chin a fraction of an inch, but her bland expression revealed nothing.

"My father is in his study. You'll have time for a cocktail before dinner if you'd care to join him," Lara suggested coolly.

"Thank you, I will." He inclined his head slightly.

With the bouquet of roses in her hand, Lara started toward the kitchen to find a vase to put the flowers in. She heard the firm strides that carried Rans MacQuade to the study door.

The few times that Rans had been to dinner before, Trevor had always been present. He was an expert at table conversation. His charm and wit always maintained a steady flow of talk among the people seated around the table.

Lara's father, on the other hand, tended to either be garrulous or silent. Unfortunately it turned out to be one of his silent nights, which left Lara with the burden of carrying the conversation. Generally she didn't find it difficult. She simply asked the necessary questions to prompt a man to talking about himself and the problem was solved.

This time she wasn't so successful. Rans MacQuade was not cooperating. He answered her questions without elaborating, as if he sensed her lack of genuine interest in his replies. His reticence was becoming irritating.

"I know much of your time is taken up with your work, but tell me, Mr. MacQuade—" Lara concealed her impatience at her role as an interviewer that had been thrust upon her "—how do you spend your free time? Obviously you hunt since you furnished Sara with tonight's quail. You must have other hobbies you enjoy, too."

"Fishing, swimming, reading, watching television—the usual pursuits." Before Lara could seize on one of the subjects, his gaze swung lazily to hold hers. "And you, Mrs. Cochran, how do you amuse yourself?"

Lara guessed immediately what he was doing. Rans MacQuade was reversing their roles, asking her the questions. The faintly mocking tone of his voice made no attempt to disguise his own lack of interest in her answers.

"The free time I do have, I usually spend horseback riding or reading. Like you, much of my time is taken up with work," she answered with cutting politeness.

"Really?" A dark eyebrow arched with sardonic disbelief.

The action scraped at her nerves. "This is a large house, Mr. MacQuade," Lara responded in a coldly defensive tone. "It requires constant attention. Sara couldn't begin to cope with all of the housework and the cooking, too."

Wry amusement danced wickedly in his eyes. "I find it difficult to visualize you scrubbing floors, Mrs. Cochran."

The comments were becoming too personal. Ignoring his remark, Lara adeptly changed the focus of attention. She smiled at her father seated at the head of the table, his dark auburn hair salted with gray.

"A good portion of my time is spent deciphering and typing daddy's notes. Now that Trevor has taken over much of the office paperwork and you, Mr. MacQuade, have taken over the management of the farm, he has finally begun to fulfill an ambition that he's had for years. I don't know if you are aware of it or not, but daddy is writing a definitive book on growing pecans."

"I'm trying, pet, I'm trying," her father corrected modestly. "I believe I mentioned it to you, didn't I, Rans?"

"You said you were doing some writing, but you didn't indicate the subject matter."

"I decided some years ago that it was time there was a book on the market that dealt with all facets of the pecan industry." Lara could see her father warming to his favorite subject and leaned back in her chair. "A composite type book that will deal with grafting and planting, diseases, methods of disease control, harvesting, marketing and the advantages and disadvantages of the known varieties—most of it from the research and knowledge I have obtained over the years."

"That is a challenging and demanding project," Rans observed.

"I'm trying to do one phase at a time," Martin Alexander explained earnestly. "Right now I'm accumulating information on the various varieties. You are more familiar with the Texas varieties. Perhaps you could give me some assistance on them."

"I'd be happy to."

A catlike smile of contentment lifted the corners of Lara's mouth. Within moments the conversation consisted of an in-depth discussion on the various merits of different varieties over others. Information and opinions were freely exchanged throughout the rest of the meal.

Once Lara accidentally encountered Rans's gaze. The satirical glitter in his eyes told her that he was aware she had manipulated the conversation to safer channels. It was disconcerting to learn that he had seen through her action so easily.

Coffee was served with the dessert. When they had finished, Lara rose from her chair, knowing if it was up to her father, the two men would linger indefinitely at the table.

"Daddy, why don't you take Mr. MacQuade into your study and offer him brandy?" she suggested.

"Excellent idea," her father agreed enthusiastically. "Will you join us, Lara?"

"No, thank you." A polite but firm smile of refusal on her lips. "I'll help Sara clear the table."

When the dishes were finished, Lara avoided the study, choosing the solitude of the living room. She wasn't really expected to join her father. He belonged to the old school that thought women should gather in one area to talk and leave the men to their important discussions. It was a decidedly archaic notion that women were incapable of intelligent conversation, but for the most part, Lara didn't care. She had reverted to the childhood practice of entertaining herself.

With a crossword puzzle in hand, she switched the television set on. The movie being televised was a sugary romance. Lara watched half of it

before impatiently turning it off. She couldn't accept, even as fiction, a love story where bells
rang and rockets soared and the couple supposedly lived happily ever after. Her experience had
made her too much of a cynic. The mystery
novel in her bedroom offered more enjoyable en-
tertainment.

As she entered the hallway, a door opened and
closed in the direction of her father's study. Lara
glanced over her shoulder and paused politely at
the sight of Rans MacQuade.

"Are you leaving, Mr. MacQuade?" She
watched the tall, muscular frame approaching. A
shiver of apprehension danced along her arms.

"Yes, I don't want to overstay my welcome,"
he answered in a low, courteous voice.

"I know how much father enjoyed discussing
his book with you, so I'm sure you couldn't do
that," Lara murmured with cool good manners.

His brown gaze flicked from her to the staircase, her obvious destination. "Were you retiring
for the night?"

"I was going to my room to read for a while."
She stiffened, uncertain why he had asked. A
smile played at the edges of his mouth as if he was
amused by the No Trespassing sign he saw in her
green eyes.

"Then I'm glad to have this opportunity to
thank you for an excellent dinner," Rans offered.

"We should thank you for the quail." This polite conversation was beginning to grate on Lara's

nerves. She wished he would say good-night and leave.

"Would it be possible for me to leave through the courtyard?" He glanced over a broad shoulder at the exit door on the opposite end of the hallway. "It's a closer walk to my cottage from there."

"You walked here?" A delicately arched brow lifted slightly. It was nearly a mile from the main house to the cottage through the pine woods.

"Yes." The wicked light in his eyes appeared to mock her surprise. "I enjoy the fresh air and exercise."

Lara chose not to comment further, but it was rare in this era of modern transportation for anyone to walk even a short distance. Instead she turned away.

"The gate is locked. I'll get the key," Lara stated.

"I don't mean to inconvenience you."

"It's no trouble," she assured him coolly.

The hall closet was concealed beneath the staircase. Pushing the latch hidden in the panel, Lara opened the door and reached for the ring of keys hanging in a far corner.

After a second's hesitation, she removed a tightly woven, black wool shawl from its hook. The night air would be cool even in February. She turned as she draped the shawl over the shimmering red gold of her hair and around her shoulders, encountering the bemused look on Rans MacQuade's chiseled face.

The tilt of her head was defiantly regal, the keys jangling in her hand. "Is something wrong, Mr. MacQuade?" Ice chilled her voice.

"Seeing you like that reminds me of the chatelaine of a castle." He seemed to lazily draw himself up another inch taller and half-turn toward the opposite end of the hallway. "Shall we go?"

With an unconscious sweep of her skirt, Lara preceded him down the hallway to the far door leading into the miniature courtyard. The Spanish-styled house was built in the shape of a blunted ∪, forming a small courtyard enclosed on three sides by the house. The fourth side was a towering brick wall to ensure privacy. The only access, except through the house, was a sturdy wrought-iron gate in an arched opening of the wall. It was kept locked at all times.

The front lawn of the house was bare of any flowering shrubbery or landscaped foliage. Loblolly and longleaf pine trees shaded the green grass with the aid of two wild magnolias. The courtyard, however, was rampant with leafy foliage that soon would be bursting into bloom. It was a cool and colorful retreat when the summer sun blazed overhead.

At night, without the benefit of light from the courtyard lanterns, it was a dark, shadowy place. The pale moonlight illuminated only the small, circular fountain in the center. Lara disliked the aura of intimacy the night created by seemingly shutting off the rest of the world. Alone she enjoyed the quiet solitude, but not with Rans MacQuade at her side.

"You have a very beautiful home, Mrs. Cochran," he observed, his step slowing to gaze about him.

"Thank you." Lara was forced by politeness to check her desire to hurry him on his way and reduce her stride to his idly strolling pace.

"It isn't often that a girl marries and doesn't have to leave home."

Warily she glanced at him. Had she detected an undertone of cynical mockery in his comment? The shadows concealed his expression and she couldn't be certain.

"As large as the house is, neither Trevor nor I thought it was practical to set up another residence," Lara found herself defending their decision. "And daddy didn't look forward to rambling about the house alone."

"I wouldn't have thought a newly married couple would consider things in the terms of practicality."

Although she couldn't see his face, she could feel his speculative gaze studying her. It was an uncomfortable sensation, like being under a microscope.

"I think you are mistaken, Mr. MacQuade. Every married couple has to find a place to live. Our choice was here."

They were near the center fountain. Moonlight streamed over his shoulder to gild her creamy white complexion with its silvery glow. The black shawl framed her oval face in a medieval fashion, highlighting her delicate bone structure and the royal carriage of her head.

"I know your father is happy with the choice." His tone became impersonal, losing its inquisitive note. "When I first came here, I was curious why a man as young and fit as your father would need a manager for the farm. He is entirely capable of running it himself. Now that I've learned about his plans for a book, I understand his heights. But don't you find it boring, or are you saying that you are content being a housewife, keeping the home-fires burning for whenever your husband comes home?"

Her frosty green eyes sliced sharply to his face in time to see the sardonic curl of his mouth as he openly mocked her. She detested his arrogance more at that moment than she had ever done before.

"My life is fulfilling," was the only reply Lara gave to his taunting question. She knew their dislike of each other was mutual.

The black grillwork of the gate was in front of them. Lara paused while inserting the key into the padlock. It turned grudgingly, then finally clicked. Loosely grasping one of the iron bars, she started to swing the gate open. It unexpectedly didn't budge and her hand slipped free of the bar as her impetus carried her a stumbling step backward.

A pair of large hands closed around her waist to

steady Lara for the instant necessary to regain her balance. Then the firm support was removed and Rans MacQuade stepped around her. There was a protesting screech of the hinges before the gate allowed itself to be pulled open by him.

"It needs oiling," he said, swinging it experimentally a few times. "I'll send someone up in the morning to see to it."

"Thank you," Lara accepted his offer with cool indifference.

He stepped through the gateway, closing it behind him. "Good night, Mrs. Cochran." There was a faintly mocking inclination of his golden brown head.

"Good night."

While she snapped the lock securely closed, Lara watched the long, lazy strides that carried him into the cobwebby shadows of the pine trees. She paused, trying to analyze that moment when his large hands had nearly spanned her slender waist. She could still feel their warm imprint. His steadying touch had been automatic and impersonal.

Her own reaction had been just as bland. She had felt nothing then, and now there was only the lingering impression of his grip. An absent smile quirked the corners of her mouth as Lara turned away from the gate.

She must remember to mention the incident in her next letter to Angie. After their visit nearly a month ago, this provided proof of her assertion that she was indifferent to a man's touch. The warmth of his hands had neither aroused her nor repulsed her. Angie had not been convinced of Lara's indifference to a man's attention. This should help change her thinking.

A breeze whispered through the pines, dancing into the courtyard to tease at the shawl around her head. Lara clutched the knitted cloth tighter around her throat and hurried toward the house before the night's chill penetrated her slight covering.

CHAPTER THREE

THE BLAZE-FACED BAY snorted and tossed his head, sidestepping spiritedly amid the straight rows of pecan trees. The barren branches almost formed an arch above the horse and rider. Green, thick grass muffled the horse's high-stepping strides.

Lara soothingly stroked the silken curve of his neck before lifting the hand to her hair. The gallop had loosened a few red gold tendrils from the French pleat. She tucked them back in place.

"There's nothing like a brisk gallop to chase away the tensions, is there, Pasha?" She laughed throatily in satisfaction as she patted the hunter's neck again. "And the weather is perfect. It feels like spring is here already, and it's only the end of February."

The sky was a brilliant blue with not a cloud or jet trail in sight. The temperature, too, was that of a balmy spring morning. The ribbed knit of her black turtleneck sweater was ample coverage, even during the cooling gallop that had carried Lara deep into the pecan orchard.

Reining the horse at a right angle, she turned him toward the distant fence and the connecting

gate to the next field. Her gaze studied the outstretched branches. Although the dogwood trees
growing wild in the pines had begun to show signs
of budding, the pecan trees remained dormant.
They generally waited until around the first official
day of spring to begin budding. Yet always it was
an event for Lara when the first shoot was seen.

As she neared the adjoining field, the decreas-
ing rows of trees enabled her to catch a glimpse of
the fence. A telltale patch of brown black contrasted with the green rye grass in this orchard,
pasture land for the cattle until the autumn har-
vest when the nuts began falling from the trees.
The furrows of brown in the next field answered
the question that Lara had been wondering about
since she had started out.

Touching the riding crop to the hunter's flanks,
she urged him into a rocking canter. Plowing had
started in the next orchard to prepare the field for
the hay crop to be planted. All the orchards served
dual purposes, first to grow pecans, and second as
grazing land or cropland.

Where there were freshly furrowed rows of dirt
on Alexander land, Cato could not be far away.
With a quick smile, Lara corrected the silent
thought—Cato and his mules couldn't be far away.
It was one of the old traditions that hadn't been cast
aside. No matter how many tractors and modern
farm machinery there were in the sheds, the plowing was always done by Cato and his mules.

As a child Lara had not questioned the custom,

spending many hours tagging along beside the tall, spare man as he walked behind his mules, always talking to them as if they could understand every word he said. Officially the mules were Alexander property. Unofficially they belonged to Cato. For sixty-seven of his eighty-two years, he had taken care of the mules and walked behind them as they plowed the fields.

Despite his advanced years, his body was not encumbered by age. He could still walk as long and as far as he had when he was thirty. With a smile, Lara remembered that last fall Cato had planted a strawberry bed for his ninety-eight-year-old mother, grumbling that the cranky old hen would probably live to see it bear fruit.

Not until Lara was sixteen did she question the wisdom of letting Cato plow the fields when tractors would be so much faster. The occasion had been brought about by the discovery that the seemingly ageless man was in fact seventy-four. She had argued with her father that surely something else could be found for Cato to do. To this day, she could vividly recall her father's response.

"Cato doesn't know anything else, pet," her father had explained patiently. "His mules are his life, and his work is his pride. After the loyalty he has shown us, surely we can return it by letting him keep his job for as long as he's capable of holding it."

"But he's worked all these years. Why don't you give him a pension and let him retire? He's certainly earned that right, too," Lara had pointed out.

"To take away Cato's mules and his pride?" He had shaken his head. "I might as well give him a gun to shoot himself with, because he wouldn't have anything else to live for."

The white boards of the fence gate glistened in front of Lara. Without dismounting, she unlatched the gate and rode through, closing it behind her. The bay's hooves ground deeply into the freshly turned soil.

A frown creased Lara's forehead. It was not the jangle of harness she heard on the other side of the knoll, but the steady hum of a tractor motor. She couldn't believe it, and turned the bay hunter down one of the straight furrows, urging him into a slow canter with a click of her tongue and a touch of the riding crop.

As she crested the small ridge, there was the tractor and plow moving steadily through the row of trees. She recognized the driver and called, meaning to find out why Cato wasn't there, but he couldn't hear her over the din of the motor.

The uneven ground made the going too difficult for the bay and Lara reined him over to the unplowed section. When they had passed the tractor, she cut across, halting the horse directly in its path and forcing the tractor to stop. The bay did not like the noisy machine and tossed its head in vigorous protest when Lara guided him alongside of it.

"Where's Cato?" she shouted to the driver.

The man cupped a hand to his ear, a curious frown on his face as his mouth formed the word "What?" Her mouth thinned into an exasperated line. Quickly she signaled to John Porter to cut the engine. It sputtered and died, the cessation of noise intensifying the peaceful silence of the orchard.

"What's the trouble, Miss Lara?" An inquiring smile curved his mouth.

"Where's Cato, John?" Lara repeated her earlier question. "Why are you doing the plowing instead of him?"

"MacQuade's orders." The man shrugged, turning his head away from her to spit out his chaw of tobacco.

"Didn't you explain to him that Cato has always done the plowing here?"

"I tried." The dubious shake of the man's head indicated it hadn't made much difference. "But he didn't seem to care how things were done before he came."

Temper flared and Lara controlled it with effort. "I will explain it to him," she said determinedly. "In the meantime, John, you can drive the tractor back to the sheds. Cato will be doing the plowing here."

The pangs of uncertainty flashed across the man's face. "MacQuade told me to plow the field," he argued hesitantly. "Your father made it very clear when MacQuade took over that he was the boss and none of us would be expected to take orders from anyone else, not even your father. It could mean my job, and my wife's going to have a baby in a couple of months. I can't risk MacQuade using me as an example to the others that he's in charge. You understand, don't you?"

"Yes." The admission was clipped out with irritation while her mind raced to find an alternate solution to achieve the same ends. "Give me the ignition key, John." She breathed in deeply. "Tell MacQuade that I stopped you and took the key. He would hardly expect you to fight with the boss's daughter to try to get it back. This way he'll see that I'm solely responsible and not blame you."

"Well," he murmured uneasily, "if you think it will work."

Lara dismounted as John Porter removed the key from the ignition and swung down from the tractor. Reluctantly he handed it to her.

"MacQuade isn't going to be happy about this." He shook his head. "You know that?"

"I can handle Mr. MacQuade," Lara asserted confidently.

There was an upward flick of his eyebrows as if John Porter wasn't too sure that Lara knew what she was talking about. He glanced at the tractor and plow.

"I suppose I might as well start back," he sighed.

"I'll walk with you." Lara fell into step beside him, leading the horse by the reins. "I might as well find Mr. MacQuade and get this mess straightened out about Cato."

The man offered no encouraging comment as they followed the brown red furrows toward the road fence. Reaching into his shirt pocket, he took out a pouch of chewing tobacco, put a pinch between his cheek and gum, then returned the pouch to his pocket.

"Would he be at the sheds?" Her inquiry broke the uneasy silence.

"At the sheds or checking one of the fields. They're plantin' some new seedlings in that acreage that was cleared last winter. He might be there," the man suggested.

Lara pressed her lips tightly together and lapsed into silence. Just thinking how carelessly Rans MacQuade had cast aside one of the valued traditions of Alexander land made her blood run hot. She cautioned herself to deal with confrontation coolly and calmly, but it was going to be difficult not to allow her personal dislike of the man to get in the way. Nor was he the type to take kindly to being ordered around by a woman. To be successful she would have to be diplomatic.

They were nearly at the fence when a pickup truck rolled into view on the graveled road, a cloud of dust following it. The pickup slowed, tires crunching on the gravel, and turned into the orchard entrance, stopping short of the gate.

John Porter darted Lara a grim look. "You aren't going to have to go looking for MacQuade."

Mentally Lara braced herself for the meeting, wishing she had been allowed a little more time to formulate what she was going to say. The truck door on the driver's side was opened, then slammed shut. Sunlight glinted on the golden highlights of Rans MacQuade's brown hair as he walked around the cab through the gate.

His gaze flicked briefly to Lara then centered on John Porter. "Did the tractor break down?"

In the outdoors he seemed taller and leaner and more rugged looking than Lara had remembered him being the few times she had seen him at the house. He was definitely a man that the workers would look up to with decided respect. She understood why John Porter was reluctant to deliberately disobey him—which didn't alter her decision at all.

"Not exactly." John Porter shuffled nervously as he tried to answer the question put to him. He paused and spat a stream of yellow tobacco juice onto the plowed ground. "You see . . . ."

He glanced expectantly at Lara. The action brought a thoughtful narrowing of Rans MacQuade's brown eyes, but they didn't waver from the man's face.

"I believe there's been a bit of a misunderstanding Mr. MacQuade," Lara inserted, coming to the man's rescue. At that point she was impaled by the hard, piercing gaze. Her fingers closed tightly around the tractor keys. "I can readily understand how it happened. You haven't been here long enough to be familiar with all of the ways we do things."

"Has this something to do with the man Cato and his mules?" Rans inquired in an ominously low voice.

"Yes." A stiff smile curved her mouth. "It is a tradition that he always plows Alexander ground. My father has stated many times that it is one that will continue for as long as Cato lives. To deprive him of his job would be the same thing as taking away his dignity and self-respect. It would hardly be the way to reward him after all his years of loyal service."

Rans MacQuade breathed in deeply and glanced away, irritation in the compressed line of his mouth. "Where's the tractor?" The question was addressed to Porter.

"About a third of the way down this row." The man gestured over his shoulder.

"I want you to go back to the tractor and—" Rans began.

"I haven't got the key," John interrupted and quickly avoided the sharp gaze that was directed at him.

"John was reluctant to stop plowing since you had ordered him to do it," Lara explained evenly. "So I took the ignition key away from him."

His jaw tightened as Rans MacQuade turned back to study her coldly. "May I have the key, Mrs. Cochran?"

There was a flash of triumph in her green

eyes. Lara concealed it with a sweep of her gold-tipped lashes. She hadn't expected him to give in so quickly. Admittedly the stressing of her father's wishes had probably resulted in her success. She extended the hand with the tractor key to him.

"I knew once it was explained to you you would understand, Mr. MacQuade," she offered graciously.

Her comment brought a sardonic twist to the ruthless line of his mouth. He took the keys and turned to John, holding them out to him.

"Here," Rans said shortly. "Enough time's been wasted. Get back on that tractor and get this orchard plowed."

Like Lara, John stared at him in stunned disbelief. With a surge of white-hot anger, Lara realized her explanation had meant nothing. She had been a fool to think she could reason with anyone as arrogantly confident as Ransom MacQuade. She had let herself be tricked into returning the key.

The riding crop hung from a strap around her wrist. During the instant when John was too surprised to reach for the keys, her fingers closed around the leather whip. Driven by her flaming temper, Lara struck out with the short whip, lashing it across the back of the outstretched hand that held the keys.

Immediately they dropped from his fingers, falling onto the plowed sod. A hissing curse accompanied the abrupt spin by Rans in her direction, the chiseled features harsh with anger. Lara's breath was coming in uneven spurts, but her expression was completely composed, with a barely challenging lift of her chin.

The air crackled with high-voltage tension. Her gaze slid to the angry red welt across the back of his hand, the fingers doubled to form a fist. She was absently aware of John glancing hesitantly from one to the other. Rans had not forgotten his presence, either.

"I left the keys in the truck, John," The smoldering glare of his eyes didn't leave Lara's face. "Drive it back to the sheds and report to Clive."

Lara did not make the mistake of interpreting his order as an admission that he was going to allow Cato to plow the fields. Rans was getting rid of John so he wouldn't witness the argument that was to come. Lara had no doubt that the gloves of politeness would come off when John left. Burning anger raged through her veins. She was in no way intimidated by him.

John spat again on the ground, glancing at her out of the corner of his eyes. He was torn between two loyalties. He had known Lara for years and was reluctant to leave her alone with Rans Mac-Quade. At the same time, he didn't want to risk losing his job since the welfare of his growing family depended on the money he brought home.

With an almost imperceptible nod of her head, Lara indicated that John should go. She was capable of fighting her own battles, even with an opponent as formidable as Rans MacQuade. Rans caught the exchange and his expression darkened as John walked toward the pickup truck parked at the gate.

The bay horse snorted nervously. Reacting to the turbulent tension in the air, he tossed his head and tugged at the reins in Lara's hand. The heavy silence continued until the pickup truck door was opened and shut and the motor growled. Lara didn't give Rans an opportunity to take the initiative.

"I don't believe you heard me correctly, Mr. MacQuade. Cato always does whatever plowing needs to be done on Alexander land. It is a long-standing tradition that not even you are going to stop."

"Let's get this straight, Mrs. Cochran." His cold voice would have made an icicle shiver. "I am the one in charge now. It makes no difference to me if your father whimsically indulged a senile old man. I have no intention of wasting precious time while an eighty-two-year-old man todders up and down a field behind some overweight mules. My concern is getting the land ready for planting in the fastest and most efficient way possible."

"What is time?" she flared. "It's a meaningless measurement. The ground, the trees, the wind, they have no conception of it. They are still here. They still exist. The efficient use of time is worthless if it means sacrificing the principles of human dignity." Green fires flashed in her eyes as she paused to catch her breath. "And you obviously have never spent any time with Cato to dismiss his worth so contemptuously. I assure you he does not todder, but strides with the physical ease that you do. His mules are always kept in condition. That's not fat but muscles you see."

"It doesn't change anything. My decision stands," Rans stated with unrelenting hardness.

A finely drawn brow arched upward. "It will stand only until my father hears about it," Lara declared haughtily. "And once the rest of the workers discover that the Alexander family does not support you in this, you will have difficulty finding anyone to do the plowing. We have always taken great pride in the loyalty of the people who work for us."

"I wouldn't be too sure about your father, if I were you, Mrs. Cochran." A self-satisfied glint appeared in his narrowed eyes. "I have already discussed the matter briefly with him and he left the final decision to me."

"That's a lie!" she gasped in sudden, trembling outrage. "My father would never condone this! He would not betray Cato in the way you are suggesting!"

One corner of his mouth quirked sardonically. "It's not betrayal," Rans harshly mocked her description. "The man will receive an ample pension to keep him comfortably for the rest of his life."

"Is that all?" Lara asked sarcastically. "Don't you want to throw in a gold watch, too?" A muscle twitched along his jaw as his lips thinned into a straight line. "Have you told Cato of your decision, or do you intend to let the grapevine inform him that he's out of a job because he's too old?"

"I haven't had the opportunity," he replied coldly.

"Oh, you've been busy I'm sure," she responded caustically. "Too busy to do the dirty work. Let Cato think my father is to blame. What does it matter to you?"

"I have been busy. Some fool forgot to latch one of the bull-pen gates and two of our prize bulls got into a fight. I'm still not certain we aren't going to lose one of them. Plus one of the cows died giving birth to a calf, and I've spent the last three nights trying to keep the calf alive. Since the decision was mine, I chose not to delegate the responsibility of informing Cato to anyone else. When I do talk to him, I will make it clear that the decision was mine."

The bay pranced nervously behind Lara, who was now trembling with the fierceness of her anger. "I am going to fight you on this, Rans MacQuade. I don't accept that your decision is the final one. You will regret it if you try to carry it out. No one who works here is going to approve of what you're doing. Believe me, I won't be fighting you alone."

"You are a spoiled little brat who has got her way too often. You can rant and rave and throw all the temper tantrums you want, but if you ever try to usurp my authority with the workers, you will find that you have tackled more than you can handle!" The fire glittering in his eyes warned that it was not an idle threat.

"I doubt that," Lara jeered.

"Do you?" A thick eyebrow arched arrogantly. "Pick up the tractor keys and hand them to me."

It was undeniably an order. Mutinously Lara stood her ground, her red gold head thrown back in open defiance, daring him to try to make her, Martin Alexander's daughter, obey.

"I said pick up the keys," he snapped.

With the swiftness of a striking cobra, his fingers wrapped around her wrist, jerking her forward. The bay reared, pulling the reins free from the same hand he held. Lara's reaction was instinctive. The riding whip arced toward that arrogant face.

The whip didn't reach its target, checked in mid-swing by another set of iron fingers seizing her other wrist. Brown eyes glinted with mockery at her futile attempt. Rigidly Lara stood in front of him, moving her wrists only slightly to test the firmness of his hold while she silently smoldered with rage.

"Let me go!" she hissed.

A hard smile curved the strong line of his mouth, his grip tightening. "So you can use that riding crop? Not a chance." Harsh, mocking laughter sounded in his throat. "If anyone uses it, I will ... on your backside. Something your father should have done years ago.''

Lara tossed her head back, green eyes glinting with confident challenge. "You wouldn't dare," she jeered.

Again a dark eyebrow flicked upward. The pressure of his grip was slightly increased, fingers digging into the delicate bones of her wrist, forcing Lara to lean forward to lessen the sharp pain.

"Wouldn't I?" Rans murmured softly.

In that split second, Lara realized that there was very little this arrogant, dominating man wouldn't dare. And she just might have goaded him into proving it. There was no way she was going to suffer that kind of humiliation at his hands.

With a quick downward twist of her wrists, she tried to surprise him and pull free, without success, but that was only the beginning of the struggle. Kicking and twisting and clawing the air around his face, Lara fought to get loose. He held her easily, amused by her vigorous efforts.

Two of the pins fell out of her hair, tousled waves of shimmering red gold curved around her cheek only partially held back by the remaining pins. Her heart was racing madly, the exertion of her struggles coloring her cheeks. Green eyes blazed with the light of battle, refusing to submit to superior strength.

Summoning what remained of her own strength, Lara stiffened her arms, straining her wrists against the overlapping of fingers and thumbs.

With a quick twist, Rans curved them behind her back, imprisoning her against the solid wall of his chest.

Her hipbones were forced against the bruising hardness of his thighs. Breathing heavily, her energy nearly spent, Lara kicked weakly at his shins with the toes of her riding boots. After a series of harmless, glancing blows, a toe accurately found its target, drawing a stifled curse near her ear.

With punishing cruelty, Rans twisted her arms higher up the curve of her spine, arching her more firmly against him. "You damned little hellcat!" he muttered savagely.

Reacting to the shooting pains in her arms, Lara jerked her head back and up. Her parted lips accidentally came in contact with his mouth. Instantly she was paralyzed, totally incapable of any movement. The scent of him enveloped her in an invisible, musky cloud. She was suddenly conscious of his shirt buttons biting into her breasts.

The same stillness gripped Rans. Less than a feather separated their lips, yet neither moved. No longer blinded by her temper, Lara couldn't ignore her vulnerability to a male assault. Frightened, her rounded eyes gazed helplessly into the brown depths of his, veiled by thick, spiky lashes. Her pulse quickened, drumming loudly in her ears. His attention seemed to be focused on the flaming disarray of her hair, then his gaze moved with unnerving slowness to look into her eyes.

For ticking seconds they were locked together,

lips touching without kissing. There was no one to hear her if she screamed. She was at his mercy and Lara doubted if he possessed any. But she wouldn't beg for it, not from him or any man.

When the seconds had stretched to a fever pitch, his grip shifted on her wrists, releasing one as he spun her away with the other. Before Lara could draw a shaky breath of relief, pressure was applied to the still captured wrist, bending her down toward the ground.

"Pick up the key," Rans growled thickly.

She had completely forgotten the cause that had precipitated her struggles moments before and stared at the ground blankly. The plowed earth bore imprints of their scuffle and the key was nowhere to be seen.

"I can't see it." Her voice trembled in humiliating betrayal.

Rans forced Lara to her knees, then joined her, raking the dirt with his fingers and uncovering the key. He picked it up himself and pulled her to her feet, his eyes glittering with a dark light. Reluctant curiosity flickered across her face as she wondered why he hadn't made her pick up the key.

"I couldn't have the chatelaine of the castle getting dirt beneath her fingernails, could I?" His mouth crooked derisively as he answered her unspoken question. There was no change in his expression when he let go of her wrist. "Unless you want to walk home, Mrs. Cochran, I suggest you go catch your horse."

Lara averted her head at his cutting sarcasm, massaging her numbed wrist and hand. When she glanced up to retort in kind, Rans MacQuade was striding down the swath of turned soil in the direction of the tractor.

Tears burned the back of her eyes and she blinked furiously to check the impulse to cry. With the back of her hand she rubbed her mouth, trying to rid her lips of the warm sensation of the nearness of his. It didn't work. They still trembled achingly in remembrance, as did the rest of her flesh where his body had been imprinted on it.

Wrenching her gaze away from the hated sight of the broad shoulders tapering to slim hips, Lara searched the orchard for the bay hunter. She glimpsed a flash of his dark, sleek coat through the branches of the trees some distance away. He appeared to be grazing, his short flight checked by the temptation of green grass.

Tapping the riding crop against her tan breeches, Lara forced her weak legs to carry her to the horse. Luckily Pasha was easy to catch. The sound of the tractor motor reminded Lara of Cato and she was filled with new purpose.

Once she caught the hunter, she would take the shortcut home through the tangled growth of pines. She was going to corner her father about his supposed endorsement of Rans MacQuade's plan to pension off Cato. She hadn't given up the fight by any means.

CHAPTER FOUR

WHEN LARA arrived at the house, it was to discover that her father wasn't home. Two or three mornings a week, depending on the workload, her father went into the office. This turned out to be one of those mornings. Sara informed her that he would be back for lunch, but Lara didn't want to wait that long before talking to him.

Her attempt to contact him at the office was thwarted by the receptionist's announcement that he had taken a prospective buyer to look over the young bulls that were for sale. Lara restlessly prowled the house, pouncing on Martin Alexander the instant he walked through the door shortly before noon.

"Well, hello, pet," he greeted her in mild, but pleased surprise when she met him at the door.

Lara dispensed with the formality of a greeting and went straight to the point. "Is it true you told MacQuade he could pension off Cato?"

Her father paused, taken aback by the sparkling fires in the green eyes of his usually calm and composed daughter. "I wouldn't put it quite that way," he frowned. "Rans discussed the possibility with me about a month ago. I made it clear that my wish was to keep him, but the decision ultimately rested with him since he is in charge."

"He chose not to consider your wishes," Lara retorted acidly. "As of this morning, Cato was forcibly retired."

"You must be mistaken." Confusion drew his sandy brows together.

"I'm not. MacQuade told me himself. Daddy—"

"But that's impossible," he interrupted. "I drove by the Desirable orchard not ten minutes ago and Cato was plowing with his mules."

"You must have been seeing things," Lara shook her head with certainty.

"Then I was hearing things, too," Martin Alexander chuckled softly, "because I stopped to ask how his mother was. He said she was just fine and that he would be stopping by in a day or two to drop off a couple of jars of his mother's fig preserves. There was no mention of retirement. You must have misunderstood Rans."

Stunned, Lara could say nothing. She knew positively that she hadn't misunderstood Rans. He had been very definite that Cato was through. She stared at her father, bewildered by his statement.

"I don't believe you," she murmured.

"Go see for yourself," he shrugged. "I imagine he's having lunch under one of the trees."

"I will," she stated flatly, opening the front door he had just closed.

"Hey, what about your lunch?"

"Tell Sara I'll have something cold when I get back," Lara replied as she closed the door.

The garage, housing her blue Mustang, was at the back of the house near the stable. Lara hurriedly followed the brick sidewalk around to the rear. Within minutes she was speeding out of the house lane behind the wheel of her car.

When she arrived at the orchard, there was definite evidence that more ground had been plowed. No sound of a motorized vehicle could be heard, which meant nothing at lunch hour. Parking the car in the orchard turn-in, Lara climbed quickly out and pushed open the gate.

Following the most recent swath of plowed soil, she walked swiftly down the row of trees, her gaze scanning the area ahead of her. She spied the mules first, standing together beneath a tree. Cato's spare frame was seated beside them, leaning against the trunk. His keen eyes saw her immediately: he lifted a weathered hand in greeting.

"Hello, Lara." He waited to continue until she was closer. "It's been a long time since you've come to walk beside old Cato." He clicked his tongue reprovingly. "You don't have a covering for your head. I told you about that time and time again. You know your skin turns as red as your hair if you get too much sun."

His words evoked fond memories that brought a smile to her lips. Lara knelt beside him, curling her legs beneath her to sit cross-legged as she had done so many times before.

"Actually, I didn't come to walk with you." She wasn't certain how she was going to explain why she came.

"You've got something troubling you. I could always tell when something was bothering you," Cato nodded sagely. "Your eyes always turn that dark shade of green, like the pines on a cloudy day."

"I never could fool you, could I?" Lara smiled wistfully, then glanced at the grass, plucking a blade and twirling it in her fingers. "Cato—" she hesitated "—did Mr. MacQuade, the new man daddy hired to run the farm—did he stop to see you this morning?"

"Hee, hee, hee!" A high-pitched chuckle rolled from a snaggle-toothed grin. "So that's it. Yep, he stopped to see old Cato."

"And?" Lara prompted as the old man shook his head as if remembering the meeting, the grin still splitting his weathered face.

"I was chopping logs, when he came, for my firewood customers," he nodded. "I knew why he'd come, a new man and all. He'd come to tell Cato he was too old to work any more."

Lara flinched at the perceptive words. "I'm sorry, Cato."

"Don't you be sorry for me," he scolded sharply. "I've lived long and hard and seen me some good times and I don't mind growing old. Not that there's a damned thing I could do about it if I did mind." The gentle smile returned, the one of a man who knows inner peace. "Well, as I was saying I knew why he'd come, but I didn't want to hear the words, not right off. So I told him I couldn't talk until I finished the chopping. He took a look at the big pile of logs I had laying there and said he'd give me a hand. I always keep a sharp ax handy in case the one I'm using gets dull, so I won't have to stop to sharpen it. I pointed it out to him and told him he was welcome to help if he was up to it."

He paused to laugh again, his dark eyes sparkling with impish glee. Lara felt her own tension lessening. She couldn't help smiling with him.

"So we chopped and we chopped and we chopped until finally that pile was all gone," Cato continued. "He was a-sweating by then. When he buried the ax in a chuck of wood, I looked at him and said, 'We ain't done. I still got that pile to do.' It wasn't as big as the first, but I think it looked bigger to him. That's when he smiled and shook his head and said to me, 'Cato, you've proved your point. I came here today to tell you that you were too old, but right now I feel older than you.' Then he told me I'd better get my mules hitched up and out to the field."

"He really said that," Lara breathed. "Oh, Cato, I'm so glad. Neither daddy nor I wanted you to retire and I hope you didn't get your feelings hurt by what happened."

"Hurt?" He straightened, drawing his head back to give her a hard look. "This is a proud day.

I wouldn't want to keep my job on any man's sufferance. I earned my right to work here today and that new man knows it or I wouldn't be here."

"You're right, of course," she agreed with a happy smile.

"That new man's going to be good. It's a pity you didn't marry someone like him instead of that skirt-chasing dandy," Cato said bluntly.

The smile vanished from her face. Hastily she got to her feet, averting her head to hide the rush of color to her cheeks. She should have realized that some gossip would have filtered through to him.

"I'd better be getting back to the house." She changed the subject hurriedly with a lie. "They're holding lunch for me."

"I'm too old to mind my own business, if that's what you're saying," he chuckled, "but I gotta get back to work now. You stop by to see me again, Lara. And bring a hat for your head."

"I will, Cato," she promised as he closed his lunch bucket and agilely rose to his feet. "Goodbye."

He lifted a hand in acknowledgement, then turned to his mules. As Lara walked away, she could hear him talking to them in a low, musical tone. A smile played on her lips. She found it amusing that Cato had got the best of Rans MacQuade. She had thought no one could change Rans's mind, but she was glad that he had. And she was glad about the way it happened.

Lara was still smiling when she reached her car. At the sound of an approaching vehicle, she glanced up with absent curiosity. Her hand remained poised on the door handle at the sight of the familiar green and white pickup. It stopped opposite her car.

A tanned arm was crooked over the open window on the driver's side. The impassively rugged face of Rans MacQuade looked at her. Thick tobacco-brown hair had been ruffled by the wind. The truck's motor was still running. The sight of him brought back all the hated memories of their morning confrontation. Her skin tingled where it had been crushed against him.

"For the record, Mrs. Cochran," he said flatly, "you didn't change my mind. Cato did."

"I don't particularly care what changed your mind," Lara began, but her retort was drowned out as he put the truck in gear and drove away, leaving a choking cloud of dust behind.

THE FIRST WEEK OF MARCH brought an explosion of spring color to the countryside. The snow-white blossoms of the flowering dogwood competed with the mauve shade of the redbud trees, their colors heightened by the contrasting backdrop of the thick pine forests of central and southern Mississippi.

In the courtyard the roses were blooming in red and pink profusion, their fragrance filling the air.

The delicate flowers of the honeysuckle vines that clung to the brick walls were a vibrant yellow, their sweet scent vying with the rose fragrance. Azaleas and camellias were budding to join in the annual rebirth of spring.

The riotous display in the miniature courtyard was artificially illuminated by the lanterns scattered in strategic locations throughout the gardened area. Light blazed from every window of the house. The tiled floor of the entrance hall was waxed to a high-gloss shine. The woodwork throughout the house gleamed with fresh polish.

Lara paused beside a hallway table to adjust a floral arrangement in a vase. Her empire gown was a daring shade of pastel pink that accented the marble creaminess of her complexion and highlighted the fiery color of her hair piled in old-world ringlets atop her head. At the sound of footsteps, she turned toward the staircase.

"Lara, would you fix my tie?" Trevor turned at the landing and came down the last set of steps, his hands fumbling with the black bow. "I can't seem to get it right."

"Of course," she agreed blandly. Trevor looked darkly elegant in his black suit and a vest of silver brocade. Now Lara could see how easily her head had been turned by his handsome looks, not the man.

While she expertly started tying the bow, she could feel his dark eyes possessively studying her.

The diamond in her wedding ring flashed brilliantly on her fingers, but Lara was no longer blinded by what it was supposed to represent.

"You are beautiful, Lara," Trevor murmured huskily. "You are an absolute vision tonight."

"Thank you," she replied politely.

"We don't really have to be here for this pilgrimage tour. Let's sneak off somewhere, just the two of us." His hands settled around her waist in suggestive familiarity.

Impatiently she pushed them away. "Stop it, Trevor."

"You are my wife, Lara. Have you forgotten that?"

"I haven't. Have you?" Her gaze flicked coldly to his face.

"You are on my mind constantly." He caressed her with his voice and eyes.

"Constantly? Don't you mean that between the blonde and the brunette you think of your wife?"

"Why must you keep bringing up the past?" He frowned. "That episode with my secretary has been over for a long time."

"Has it?" Lara smiled cynically. "Or have you merely replaced her with someone else?"

His dark, nearly black eyes narrowed harshly. "If I have, can you honestly blame me?" Trevor challenged. "I have normal physical needs, obviously unlike you. You were the one who shut me out, Lara. It isn't my fault that I have to go outside my marriage to seek satisfaction."

"That's a pat explanation." Lara knotted the bow. "Unfortunately it doesn't hold true for your first affair with the blonde. At least, I presume it was the first," she added tautly.

"I was a fool. I admit it." His arms slid around her waist before she could stop them. His hands locked together at the small of her back and he drew her against him. "You are still the most beautiful woman in my life. All I'm asking is another chance to make you the happiest." Trevor bent his dark head to nuzzle her ear, ignoring the rigidity of her body. "Once you enjoyed having me make love to you. I can make you feel good again. Let me show you tonight, darling. We can slip away to some intimate little spot, drink some champagne and dance. We did that on the first night of our honeymoon, remember? And I carried you all the way up to our hotel room?"

Lara remembered. But that girl in his arms had been someone else. She closed her eyes. Every nerve in her body now seemed to be dead at his touch.

"Let me go, Trevor," she said tautly. "Save your romantic words and kisses for some other gullible fool. I'm not interested in them anymore."

"I'm not going to accept that," Trevor murmured against the corner of her unresponsive mouth. "In time you'll change your mind and admit that you want me."

"You're wrong, Trevor. Now let me go," Lara commanded in a low voice.

"Okay, you two lovebirds, break it up." Her father's affectionately chiding voice joined them in the entry hall. "The tour will be here any time now."

Knowing Lara would not openly resist him in her father's presence, Trevor took advantage of the embrace to claim her lips in a possessive kiss before releasing her. Lara accepted it with cold tolerance, straightening the edges of his bow tie, then walked calmly away, the soft material of her long gown swishing around her ankles.

"The house looks as marvelous as you do, Lara," Martin Alexander declared.

"She is beautiful, like a goddess," Trevor agreed, his dark eyes glowing as he looked at her.

Her lips curved with the semblance of a smile at the compliment she knew was insincere. At the first sound of activity in the driveway outside, Lara turned toward the front door.

"I believe the tour is arriving now." Trevor was immediately at her side when she opened the door to admit the group. His hand rested on her waist, acting out the part of a romantic and happy wedded couple.

It was going to be a long and trying evening, Lara thought silently, if Trevor was going to take advantage of the touring guests to make his unwanted advances. There was very little she could do about it as she welcomed the guests to their home.

As usual, the group consisted mainly of couples. There was a trio of elderly women, who were obviously friends, and a representative of the Hattiesburg Historical Society. Lara was mildly surprised to see a young, attractive brunette in the group. She supposed she was the daughter of one of the couples.

The woman was staring at Trevor. A fact that didn't surprise Lara. It would have surprised her more if the brunette hadn't taken notice of him. Her dark gaze shifted to Lara, envy flashing across her face. Lara smiled faintly and looked away. If the woman only knew, she thought wryly, how totally false the impression was that she and Trevor were a happily married couple, she would probably be shocked.

Quietly Lara remained at Trevor's side, listening to her father as he explained to the group the details and the dimensions of the house and some of its early history. He was proud of his home and enjoyed showing it to visitors. He had just invited the group to follow him into the living room when there was a knock at the door.

Lara used the interruption as an excuse to separate herself from Trevor. "You go ahead with the others. I'll answer the door."

She had partially expected him to protest, but he smiled an acceptance and followed the group into the living room. With a little sigh of relief and a flicker of curiosity as to the identity of the late caller, she walked to the door and opened it.

Rans MacQuade was framed by the opening, vitally masculine in a crisp white shirt, opened at the throat, and dark trousers. She had seen him only a few times since the incident with Cato, then only at a distance. Fingers curled into the palm of her hand, her head tilting to a faintly haughty angle.

His lazy yet very alert brown eyes noticed the instinctive reaction with sardonic amusement. His gaze moved insolently over the perfection of her features, traveling down her slender neck to the hollow of her throat. It didn't stop there, but continued over the bareness of her skin, halting for an instant on her grandmother's brooch that modestly concealed the shadowy cleft between her breasts, then swept over the clinging material of her gown.

Her skin burned as if he had physically touched her. Lara's green eyes flashed her dislike of his insulting inspection when his gaze returned to her face.

From the living room came the chattering of several voices. Lara guessed that her father had invited the group to ask questions. Rans Mac-Quade heard them, too, and glanced in the general direction of the living room, hidden from his view by the house walls.

"I'm sorry. I wasn't aware you were entertaining this evening," he apologized smoothly.

"Not entertaining, exactly," Lara corrected in a coolly distant tone. "This is the night of the candlelight tour in connection with the annual pilgrimage. Was it something important you wanted?"

"No." Rans shook his head, a glint of curiosity entering his eyes. He raised his left hand slightly to indicate the thick folder he was carrying. "I promised Martin last week that I would gather the notes and literature I had on the Texas varieties of pecans. I finished about an hour ago and decided to bring them over."

"If you'd like, you can leave them in his study," Lara suggested, opening the door wider to admit him into the house. "I'm sure he'll want to go over them with you another evening when you are both free."

"I'll contact him tomorrow." Rans stepped into the hallway, his gaze idly sweeping into the living room where guests were trailing into the adjoining area. "Did you say it was a tour? I'm sorry," he offered with a trace of curious confusion, "but I wasn't aware that your home was open to the public."

"It isn't, with the exception of Pilgrimage Week."

Lara escorted him down the hallway toward the study. She was strangely reluctant to let him linger in the house longer than it was necessary to deliver the papers he had brought.

"Pilgrimage. Is that a local festivity?"

"Various cities throughout the state and the South have what is referred to as a pilgrimage.

scheduled at various times in the year. It's an annual event of the Hattiesburg Historical Society, which arranges for private homes that are historically significant to be open to the public on a tour basis. Most of the tours are in the afternoon, but certain homes are viewed in the evening in what is referred to as a candlelight tour," Lara explained in a concise tone.

"Historically significant?" An eyebrow arched inquiringly.

"In our case, it's more the unusual architecture of the house than famous personages or events. Generally the architecture of southern plantation homes is Greek Revival or colonial. Many homes are full of valuable antiques. Our appeal is mainly the heavy Spanish influence and the picturesque courtyard within the house walls."

"Doesn't it bother you to have a group of strangers parading through your home?" He closed the door, his gaze focusing curiously on her face.

"It's only once a year," she smiled coolly, "not an everyday occurrence. Besides, my father enjoys it." Lara glanced pointedly at the large mahogany desk nestled in front of filled bookshelves. A large chair covered in wine-colored leather was behind it. "You can put the papers on his desk."

The tall windows in the study were actually paned glass doors opening into the courtyard, as in every room on the lower floor except the living room and side parlor. Heavy velvet draperies in a matching wine color flanked the doors. The draperies were open, providing a view of the softly lighted courtyard.

As Rans passed the windowed doors to put the papers on the desk, he glanced out. "I had hoped to use the courtyard gate again, but your tour group is out there."

"They'll be coming inside in a few minutes to see the parlor and the study before daddy takes them upstairs."

"They actually go through your private rooms, too?" he mocked.

"No, only the two guest rooms and daddy's sitting room," she answered stiffly, glancing through the window to see the visitors begin filing toward the door leading into the entrance hall. "They're coming back into the house now."

"Is the gate locked?"

"Yes, it is." Lara was angry with herself for forgetting that. "Excuse me, I'll get the key."

She slipped quickly into the hallway. The tour group was slowly congregating inside the rear area of the hall, waiting for the stragglers still gazing around the garden. In the buzz of conversation, Lara's quiet trip to the closet and back to the study went unnoticed.

Rans was leaning a hip against the side of the desk, his arms folded in front of him when she returned. He straightened with lazy nonchalance as she closed the door and walked swiftly toward the glass-paned doors.

"I should apologize for keeping you from the tour," he offered.

"It's quite all right. Daddy usually takes over, anyway." Lara shrugged the polite gesture aside.

The door latch turned silently in her hand. She started to walk through the opening when she heard a woman's voice in the courtyard. She hesitated for a fraction of a second, not wanting to encounter the tour group, then decided it didn't matter whether she did or not. A step later, she froze at the sound of Trevor's voice.

"Darling, you took such a chance coming here like this," he whispered. "What were you thinking about?"

The voice was close to the study, but wherever Trevor was, he and the girl must have been concealed in the shadows, because Lara strained her eyes and could see nothing.

"I had to see you. It's been so long," the girl murmured with an aching throb in her voice. "I couldn't help it. I had to come."

"I know," Trevor responded. "I've been wanting to see you, too, but someone from the tour is going to notice you aren't with them and come looking for you."

Lara's stomach lurched as she realized the girl had to be the attractive brunette she had noticed earlier. Her hand spread its fingers across her stomach to check its sickening turn.

"Not for a few minutes," the brunette protested. "Oh, Trevor, darling, you never told me your wife was so very beautiful. I wanted to die when I saw the two of you together. I wanted to tear the ring from her finger and tell the world that you belonged to me, but she's so much more beautiful than I am." The torture of jealousy and envy vibrated her words.

"Lara is beautiful, yes," Trevor agreed, "but so is an ice carving. To me, she will never be as beautiful as you are. I swear it's the truth, Melinda, love. All evening, until I saw you walk through that door, I kept trying to find some way, some excuse, not to take part in this tour so that I could slip away and be with you tonight."

Remembering his ardent pleas to spend a romantic evening with her, Lara sunk her teeth into her lip to check the gasp that rose in her throat at his audacious lie. Trevor had certainly found another gullible fool.

"It must have been knowing how much you wanted to be with me that brought me here tonight," the girl murmured. "Darling, hold me. Hold me for just a little while."

A silence followed, faintly broken by the rustle of clothing. Lara knew they were embracing. A nauseous chill raced over her skin. Her husband was in the courtyard of their home, kissing and caressing another woman. Lara pivoted back into the study, not wanting to hear any more sounds or words of the disgusting scene.

She spun into the hard wall of Rans MacQuade's chest. In her shock at finding Trevor in the garden with another woman, she had completely forgotten that anyone else had overheard what she had. The discovery paralyzed her for a humiliating second, long enough for Rans to reach around her and close the study door to the courtyard.

"You look pale, Mrs. Cochran," he observed sardonically. "Surely you weren't surprised by what you heard. You've known all along about your husband's other women."

The pallor disappeared immediately in a flood of warmth. The words formed on her tongue to deny his statement, but it seemed pointless to deny the truth.

"I foolishly believed he would be considerate enough not to meet them in my home," Lara retorted, lifting her chin in regal scorn.

His mouth quirked into a crooked, cyncial line. "Perhaps if you were as passionate and loving as the young woman in the courtyard, Trevor would not be having these affairs. A man doesn't enjoy making love to an unfeeling marble statue, however aesthetically beautiful it is."

There was an itch in the palm of her hand to feel the stinging contact with his strong jaw. It was checked by the impulse to hurl the bitter facts of her marriage in his mocking face. There was no point in insisting that she was once passionate. Trevor's male ego would never allow him to be faithful. He constantly had to prove his manhood. He couldn't ignore the challenge of a pretty face, regardless of his love life at home. Lara obeyed neither impulse.

"I don't recall requesting any personal advice from you, Mr. MacQuade," she said icily. "Would you please leave through the front door?"

The corners of his mouth twitched in dry amusement, carving brief grooves in his lean cheeks to signify the presence of his dimples.

"I'll see myself out." His brown eyes glinted wickedly. "Good night, Mrs. Cochran."

CHAPTER FIVE

THE BRUNETTE HAD BEEN with the tour group when Lara had rejoined it. The girl had looked flushed and radiant and faintly triumphant as she met Lara's glance. Trevor had evidently reinforced his ardent words with affectionate deeds.

Almost a week had passed since the pilgrimage night. Lara might have been able to push from her mind the events of that night if it wasn't for the knowledge that Rans MacQuade had witnessed her humiliation. She knew it would be there in his eyes the next time she met him, mocking her, questioning her womanhood.

The knowledge was an irritant to her pride. Thus far, circumstances had not created a meeting. When they did, she wondered if she could contain her temper and treat him with the arrogant disdain he deserved.

Her finger turned the page of the book in her hand. Impatiently Lara flipped it back. Her eyes had skimmed the printed page, but none of the contents had registered. What was the use? Lara closed the book with a snap, rising restlessly to her feet and walking to the front window in the living room.

"Don't you like the book?" Trevor inquired, glancing up from his own. "I read it last week and found it very absorbing."

Lara stared out the window at the blackened landscape. This was one of Trevor's duty evenings that he spent at home with her to maintain his image of a devoted spouse—for her father's benefit, she supposed. She doubted if her father guessed how totally empty their marriage had become.

"When do you find time for so much reading, Trevor?" she remarked cynically.

He either didn't hear or ignored the cutting barb in her question. "It's the speed-reading course I took. Novels that used to take me days to read now take only hours, sometimes minutes depending on their length. You should sign up for the course."

"No, thank you." Lara sighed, choosing to reply directly to his suggestion and not pursue a course of condemning insults. "I don't care to read that fast. In a well-written book you would miss the passages where an author weaves the words together to create a spell. You might absorb the gist of it, but you would lose the magic. And when a book is good, I like to prolong reaching the end as long as possible."

"Is that why you've stopped reading—to prolong the end?" Trevor teased.

A wry grimace flashed across her face. She should have known he wouldn't understand what she meant. Lara wondered if he read because it was the expected thing for an educated man to do as opposed to reading for the enjoyment of it.

Glancing over her shoulder, Lara indifferently noted the way the blue shade of Trevor's short sleeved pullover accented the blue black highlights in his hair.

"I couldn't concentrate," Lara replied with a restless shrug. "I'm not in the mood to read, I guess."

A speculative gleam entered his dark eyes as he watched her. Thoughtfully Trevor closed his book. "Was there something you would rather do?" he asked with studied casualness.

Lara shook her head. "No."

Nonchalantly Trevor rolled to his feet, and strolled toward the window where she stood. "It's a beautiful evening for a drive through the country."

Impatiently she walked away from him. "I'm not in the mood."

"Poor Lara." He followed her, a smile of amusement flashing across his mouth. "You really don't know what's bothering you, do you?"

Folding her arms in front of her, she jerkily rubbed her elbows and the bareness of her upper arms. "Nothing's bothering me. I'm simply not in the mood to read."

"Something's causing your agitation," Trevor murmured huskily. "And I think I know what it is, even if you won't admit it."

"I don't know what you are talking about," Lara declared sharply, not liking his sly innuendos.

"You are as susceptible as the rest of us to the physical urge to be caressed and loved, no matter how hard you try to suppress it. It's surfacing now with your restlessness. Inwardly you are reaching out for something to satisfy you, although consciously you won't admit it."

Involuntarily Lara listened to his softly spoken words. The stirrings of dissatisfaction she felt within, the vague feelings that she was incomplete, indicated that Trevor might possibly be right about their cause. Lara firmly told herself that even if it was true, she could control them. She ruled her flesh, not the other way around.

"Is that what you think?" Lara laughed hollowly. "How disillusioning it will be to you when you find out that a cigarette will cure my unrest."

As she reached for the cigarette case sitting on the table, Trevor's hand shot out to stop her, turning Lara to face him and taking hold of her shoulders.

"I'm right. I know I am," he said.

His gaze moved suggestively over her feminine figure while his hands began to languidly caress her shoulder blades. Lara didn't move as he came close, his hands moving down her spine. He aroused only indifference, but his male ego was confident of his ability to make her respond.

"Lara," he whispered, and let his lips trail along the cord of her neck to her earlobe. "You are more beautiful than any woman I know. Darling, I want to be with you tonight."

The hypocrisy of his words produced a reaction that his caress had not. Violently she twisted away from his exploring mouth. Her expression was a cold mask of utter rejection. His words too closely paralleled the things he had said to the brunette.

"Don't touch me!" Lara hissed. "I can't stand to have your hands on me!"

Trevor stared at her in disbelief, an angry frown gathering together his dark brows. He couldn't believe she honestly found his caress repulsive.

As Lara's cold green eyes started to move their attention away from Trevor's face, they saw the tall figure standing in the entry hall outside the living-room doors. It was Rans MacQuade. How long had he been there? And how much had he overheard? All of it, Lara decided bitterly, judging from the sardonic expression in the brown eyes that held her gaze.

What was he doing in the house? How did he get in without being heard? He appeared to be coming from her father's study. Perhaps he had arrived shortly after dinner when she had been in the kitchen helping Sara with the evening dishes.

If that was true, then Rans had been on his way out of the house when he had seen Lara with Trevor in the living room. Her lips tightened. He had probably heard the nature of their conversation and paused to see if Lara was going to follow his unwarranted advice and passionately welcome Trevor's advances.

He had seen her reaction. He didn't even have the grace to look sorry or guilty that he had been eavesdropping. Angrily Lara spun away from his glittering eyes, turning away from Trevor at the same time.

"What is wrong with you, Lara?" Trevor said finally, exhaling a heavy sigh of anger and confusion.

She glanced over her shoulder, her gaze first seeking the figure in the hall. There was no one there. In the next second she heard the front door softly closing.

Her gaze flicked to Trevor. "Nothing is wrong with me. I've simply stopped believing lies, that's all. Excuse me, I'm going to my room," Lara concluded, and Trevor didn't question her answer or her decision to leave the room. It was as if he sensed that she had seen through him and didn't want to be confronted with it.

In the days that followed, Trevor didn't press his attentions on her, virtually ignoring her when they were alone. Lara decided he was trying a new ploy, hoping to gain her interest by showing none in her. He could play all the games he wanted to play, but he played them alone.

Rans MacQuade was at the house several times, conferring with her father. Outside of a few courteous exchanges, usually in the company of her father, Lara hadn't had to suffer any of his personal remarks about her life and herself.

His visits had produced a surge of writing by her father, filling Lara's time with typing his copious notes. A stranger to his methods would have found his notes impossible to follow since there were constant arrows, asterisks and amendments that had to be deciphered and inserted in the right places.

Her father was in the study this evening, going over what she had typed today and no doubt filling another tablet for more to be done tomorrow. Lara turned the hand-held hair dryer onto her face, letting the hot air blow over her skin.

The night air was so heavy with humidity that she felt as sticky as she had before she had taken a shower and washed her hair. It could have been summer outside instead of spring. She ran testing fingers through her shiny hair. There was only a trace of dampness at the back of her head.

Turning off the dryer, she put it back in its box and carried it to the closet. Lara paused at the open window overlooking the pine woods at the rear of the house. A faint breeze gently stirred the needles, hardly a breath of it entering the room. A moth beat its wings against the screen, seeking the light from her bedside lamp.

With so much typing to do for her father, Lara hadn't been out of the house in the last few days except to take care of her horse. Usually she took time out for a morning ride on the bay hunter,

Pasha, but the horse had sprained a muscle in his left front leg the last time Lara had ridden him.

There had been little swelling in the leg. Cato had looked at it and given Lara some foul-smelling liniment to put on it, decreeing that the hunter would be all right in a week or so. Cato was almost as knowledgeable as a veterinarian when it came to the equine species of animals.

With a sigh, Lara decided it was much too hot to even attempt sleep. Untying the sash of her robe, she walked to the closet and took out a pair of Levis and a white cotton blouse. She would walk to the stable and check on Pasha. Perhaps the night air would be cooler.

She opened the lingerie drawer of her dresser and closed it again without removing anything. When she had changed into the Levis and blouse, she turned to the mirror, winding her freshly washed hair atop her head. It was as slippery as silk, sliding through the pins that tried to hold it in place. Giving up, Lara secured it at the back of her neck with a tortoise-shell clasp.

Trevor was out that evening and her father was in his study working. There was no sign of Sara as Lara slipped out the front door. Few lights shone from the windows of the house, making it look dark and empty.

Stuffing her hands in the pockets of her Levis, she strolled along the brick sidewalk. The dense shadows from the pines made her feel very much alone. Only a few stars glittered through the treetops that blocked out all but the moon's halo. It wasn't much cooler but the air was fresh.

The bay whickered curiously as Lara opened the stable door and switched on the light. The building was small, with stalls for three horses plus a tack and feed room. Pasha was the only occupant. Her father had owned a horse at one time, but he had never been much of a horseman. When age had claimed his mount, he hadn't bothered to get another.

The horse stretched his blazed face toward her, nuzzling her shirt buttons as Lara rubbed his forelock. She crooned softly to him, meaningless words that were meant to soothe. A large mound of loose hay lay at the bottom of the ladder to the loft. She scooped up an armful and put it in the manger.

Leaning on the stall door, Lara studied the horse as he turned his attention to the hay. He was still favoring it slightly, not putting all of his weight on the front leg. Another application of liniment would help, she decided, and walked to the tack room and took the brown bottle from the medicine cabinet.

"Whew!" she breathed, making a face as she uncorked the bottle. "I'm going to have to take another bath when I get through putting this on you, Pasha."

As Lara reached to unlatch the lower half of the stall door, the stable door opened. She turned with a start to see Rans MacQuade filling the opening.

For a split second he paused there, his gaze·raking the length of her body.

"What do you want?" Lara demanded, frostily meeting his look.

"I noticed the light was on and stopped to see if anything was wrong," he replied evenly.

"Not a thing," she retorted, but he stepped into the stable anyway and closed the door. His presence dominated the concrete corridor, making the quarters seem closer than they actually were. "I said nothing was wrong."

"What's the matter with your horse?" Rans was completely ignoring her answer.

As he walked toward her, Lara was nearly overwhelmed by an impulse to retreat. It was crazy. There was no reason to be intimidated by him.

"Nothing is the matter with my horse, Mr. MacQuade." She steadfastly held her ground, forced to tilt her head back slightly to look directly into his face when he stopped in front of her.

He held her look for an instant then let his gaze slide lazily to the bottle in her hand. Her knuckles were turning white from gripping it so tightly, a betrayal of the wary tension that claimed her.

"What's the bottle for if nothing is the matter with your horse?" Rans mocked.

A flash of anger raced through her veins, but Lara checked it to reply calmly. "Pasha has a slight sprain, but I assure you it's nothing serious. I thought I'd put some liniment on it."

"I'll do it for you." His hand closed around the bottle, his fingers touching hers.

Lara's first instinct was to jerk her hand away from the burning contact and let him have the bottle, but she wouldn't give in to such a display of weakness.

"No, thank you. I'm quite capable of taking care of my own horse," she refused, not relinquishing her viselike hold on the bottle.

"I'm sure you are, but the odor coming from this bottle hardly smells like perfume," Rans drawled lazily. "I wouldn't want the lady of the castle to have to take two baths in one night."

Her head jerked back as betraying warmth rushed to her cheeks. "What do you mean?" she demanded stiffly, wondering how he could possibly know she had stepped from the shower barely an hour ago.

Dark, spiky lashes veiled the wicked gleam in his velvet brown eyes as they roamed with insolent thoroughness over her shining hair and face, moving down her cotton blouse. The material clung to her sticky skin, outlining the rounded fullness of her bare breasts. Flames licked her skin where he had undressed her with his eyes. Her breath came in agitated spurts of barely controlled temper.

He knew she was outraged by his action. It sparkled like a jewel fire in her eyes. Her reaction amused him, as if he had done it deliberately to get a rise from her.

"You have the fragrance of scented soap, Mrs. Cochran. It was only a guess. But an accurate one, wasn't it?" Rans taunted lowly.

Lara tore her hand away from the bottle, her arms held rigidly straight at her side. "Put the liniment on if you like," she said with a freezing dislike. "Then please get out of here."

The line of his mouth quirked mockingly as she stepped away from the stall gate to let him enter. The bay's ears pricked at the stranger. For once in his well-mannered life, Lara wished her horse would decide to bite. It wasn't to be.

The caressing deepness of Rans MacQuade's voice seemed to assure the horse that the man meant him no harm, and the bay submitted readily to the stroking firmness of the hand on his sleek neck.

"The left front?" Rans inquired, running a hand along the horse's withers and across his chest.

"Yes," was Lara's clipped answer.

Ducking under the horse's neck, Rans moved to the left side, squatting to run an exploring hand over the injured leg. The bay shifted uneasily as he probed the sore area.

"Hold his head for me, will you?" It wasn't a request.

Loathing the necessity to obey, she reluctantly took hold of the halter, crooning softly to settle him down. "Cato has already examined him," she said when Rans continued testing the extent of the injury.

He poured some of the liniment on the leg, and the powerful odor filled the air. "I'd say this is one of Cato's homemade remedies," he muttered, turning his head away.

Lara concealed a smile, knowing how vilely strong the liniment was from her own experience. For several minutes Rans rubbed the liniment in while she held the bay's head. Finally he straightened, patting the horse on the haunches as he walked around him to the stall door.

"That ought to do it," he remarked absently. "Where's the top to this?"

Mutely Lara pointed to the cork balanced on a wide manger board. He stuffed it in the bottle top and glanced inquiringly at her.

"Where does it go?"

"In the medicine chest in the tack room. I'll put it away," she answered.

He handed it to her without voicing any objection. Lara took it, carefully avoiding any accidental contact with his hand. As she started toward the tack room on the opposite side of the corridor, Rans followed. It was in the same direction as the stable door.

When he followed her into the tack room, she realized he wasn't leaving. The medicine chest was just inside the door. Lara stopped in front of it, tilting her head to a challenging angle as she turned to confront Rans.

The words to dismiss him formed on her lips, but he walked by her without a glance straight to

IT'S FUN! IT'S FREE!
AND IT COULD MAKE YOU A

MILLIONAIRE

If you've ever played scratch-off lottery tickets, you should be familiar with how our games work. On each of the first four tickets (numbered 1 to 4 in the upper right) there are Pink Metallic Strips to scratch off.

Using a coin, do just that—carefully scratch the PINK strips to reveal how much each ticket could be worth if it is a winning ticket. Tickets could be worth from $10.00 to $1,000,000.00 in lifetime money.

Note, also, that each of your 4 tickets has a unique sweepstakes Lucky Number . . . and that's 4 chances for a **BIG WIN!**

FREE BOOKS!

At the same time you play your tickets for big prizes, you are invited to play ticket #5 for the chance to get one or more free books from Harlequin®. We give away free books to introduce readers to the benefits of the Harlequin Reader Service®.

Accepting the free book(s) places you under no obligation to buy anything! You may keep your free book(s) and return the accompanying statement marked "cancel." But if we don't hear from you, then every month, we'll deliver 6 of the newest Harlequin Presents® novels right to your door. You'll pay the low subscriber price of just $2.49* each—a saving of 30¢ apiece off the cover price! And there's no charge for shipping and handling!

Of course, you may play "THE BIG WIN" without requesting any free books by scratching tickets #1 through #4 only. But remember, that first shipment of one or more books is FREE!

PLUS A FREE GIFT!

One more thing; when you accept the free book(s) on ticket #5, you are also entitled to play ticket #6, which is GOOD FOR A GREAT GIFT! Like the book(s), this gift is totally free and yours to keep as thanks for giving our Reader Service a try!

So scratch off the PINK STRIPS on all your BIG WIN tickets and send for everything today! You've got nothing to lose and everything to gain!

Here are your BIG WIN Game Tickets, worth from $10.00 to $1,000,000.00 each. Scratch off the PINK METALLIC STRIP on each of your Sweepstakes tickets to see what you could win and mail your entry right away. (SEE OFFICIAL RULES IN BACK OF BOOK FOR DETAILS!)

This could be your lucky day – GOOD LUCK!

1

THE BIG WIN

Scratch PINK METALLIC STRIP to reveal potential value of this ticket if it is a winning ticket. Return all game tickets intact.

LUCKY NUMBER

5B 641048

2

THE BIG WIN

Scratch PINK METALLIC STRIP to reveal potential value of this ticket if it is a winning ticket. Return all game tickets intact.

LUCKY NUMBER

7W 628642

3

THE BIG WIN

Scratch PINK METALLIC STRIP to reveal potential value of this ticket if it is a winning ticket. Return all game tickets intact.

LUCKY NUMBER

2F 636935

4

THE BIG WIN

Scratch PINK METALLIC STRIP to reveal potential value of this ticket if it is a winning ticket. Return all game tickets intact.

LUCKY NUMBER

6I 652026

5

FREE BOOKS

We're giving away brand new books to selected individuals. Scratch PINK METALLIC STRIP for number of free books you will receive.

AUTHORIZATION CODE

130107-742

6

FREE GIFT

We have an outstanding added gift for you if you are accepting our free books. Scratch PINK METALLIC STRIP to reveal gift.

AUTHORIZATION CODE

130107-742

YES! Enter my Lucky Numbers in THE BIG WIN Sweepstakes, and when winners are selected, tell me if I've won any prize. If PINK METALLIC STRIP is scratched off on ticket #5, I will also receive one or more FREE Harlequin Presents® novels along with the FREE GIFT on ticket #6, as explained on the opposite page.

(U-JDA-01/92) 106 CIH ADLT

NAME _____

ADDRESS _____ APT. _____

CITY _____ STATE _____ ZIP _____

Offer limited to one per household and not valid to current Harlequin Presents subscribers.
© 1991 HARLEQUIN ENTERPRISES LIMITED.

PRINTED IN U.S.A.

FOLD AND DETACH ALONG THIS DOTTED LINE—RETURN ALL GAME TICKETS INTACT.

the work sink on the far wall. Pressing her lips tightly together, Lara faced the medicine cabinet, listening to the sound of rushing water from the tap as he washed the liniment from his hands.

"I noticed the light on in the study when I walked by the courtyard." Rans turned off the faucets. "Is your father working tonight?"

"He's hardly stopped in the last few days." Lara set the liniment bottle on the shelf and closed the cabinet.

"That means a lot of typing for you," he remarked, drying his hands on a towel and hanging it over its rack.

"Yes, it does." She removed the curry rake and brush from their hooks and walked into the corridor.

Grooming the hunter would be an excuse to remain in the stable when Rans left. Impatiently Lara waited in the corridor while he took his sweet time about joining her.

"Do you resent it?" He stopped in the doorway, leaning a hand against its frame and lazily studying her marble smooth face.

Why didn't he take the hint that she wanted him to leave—quickly? The answer flickered that he probably had taken the hint and was lingering just to irritate her. He was succeeding.

"Resent what?" Briefly Lara inspected his tanned features, roughly chiseled in aggressively male lines.

Tobacco-brown hair waved with thick carelessness on his forehead. His white shirt was opened at the throat, accenting the sun-browned column and revealing the curling golden brown hairs on his chest. Muscles rippled beneath his shirt. His masculinity seemed to wrap around her with suffocating intensity.

"The book demands a lot of your father's time. It doesn't leave him much to spend with you," Rans replied.

An eyebrow arched haughtily. "I'm a big girl now, Mr. MacQuade. I no longer need to be entertained by my daddy."

"Nor by your husband, it would seem," he suggested dryly.

Breathing in sharply, Lara checked the flow of temper and allowed a sugar-coated smile to curve her lips. "That's correct, Mr. MacQuade."

"Where is your husband tonight?" He tilted his head curiously to the side, sardonic amusement glittering behind the lazily veiled lashes.

"He's part of a foursome that plays golf every Wednesday after work. They have dinner and drinks at the club afterward. A weekly 'boys' night out,'" she answered coolly.

"Do you believe that?" The grooves deepened around his mouth.

"Does it matter?" Lara challenged.

"Not to me." The wide shoulders lifted in an indifferent shrug. "I was wondering if it mattered to you."

"Not in the slightest." She studied the polished

enamel on her fingernails, wishing they didn't itch with the desire to scratch that arrogantly mocking expression from his face.

"You must sleep in a very cold bed, Mrs. Cochran." His voice laughed at her as he slowly straightened.

Lara tipped her head back, the overhead light flaming over her hair at the new angle. Boldly she met his challenging look, not intimidated by his superior height as he towered before her.

"And your bed—what's it like, Mr. Mac-Quade?" she jeered with a freezing scorn.

A wicked gleam danced in his brown eyes with seductive overtones. "Would you like to find out?"

"That's a typical male response," she laughed abruptly. "You men are so convinced that you are great lovers that you never realize how miserably you fail."

"And you feel your husband failed?" Rans inquired, a brow quirking.

"Miserably," Lara answered evenly.

"The solution is simple. Get a divorce instead of prolonging the cold war."

Pride drew her up another inch. "Alexanders don't get divorces, Mr. MacQuade," she informed him.

"Another tradition of long-standing," he mocked. "And so they lived miserably ever after." He eyed her cynically. "An Alexander makes a wrong decision, and he lives with it the rest of his life without a second chance, a martyr to tradition."

"I'm not interested in a second chance, as you put it. Once is enough for me," Lara declared loftily, the tip of her nose tilting slightly upward in disdain.

"So you remain married, drifting into a series of bitter affairs," Rans concluded with a taunting curl of his lip.

"I'll leave the affairs to Trevor. He already has the experience." Bitterness coated her tongue.

"While you hold yourself aloof from the animal desires that plague the rest of mankind. What a waste of such womanly beauty."

His sarcastically thoughtful gaze held hers, blinding her to the movement of his hand as it reached up to touch the smoothness of her cheek at his last comment. Quickly she pushed his hand away as if his fingertips had burned her skin.

"Don't touch me!" she snapped.

"I had forgotten," Rans chuckled in amusement. "You don't want a man's hands on you, do you?" He reminded Lara that he had witnessed the scene between her and Trevor. "Are you afraid you might like-it?"

"Never!" Lara hissed.

The sun lines at the corners of his eyes crinkled at her defiant challenge. "Never?" he murmured mockingly.

He took a step toward her. Feeling menaced, Lara swung the curry rake at his face. His fingers closed over her wrist, twisting it until she was forced to drop her weapon. With a jerk she was pulled against his chest, his arms sliding around her waist. She wedged a breathing space with her elbows.

"You are a vengeful little spitfire," Rans laughed huskily.

"Let me go!" Lara glared at him coldly.

She had learned in the orchard that it was useless to struggle against his superior strength. She did not intend to demean herself by trying the same tactic again.

He seemed content to hold her captive and examine the smoldering temper in her expression. "A friend asked me once to break a bad-tempered filly he had. The secret was that she needed a lot of handling sometimes with gentle roughness to remind her who was boss. Mostly she had to learn that a man's touch really wasn't so bad," he mused softly.

"I am not a filly," she retorted, inwardly frightened by the dark glint in his eyes. "Let me go."

Rans merely smiled, lean dimples appearing in the tanned cheeks. Lara breathed in sharply as his hands moved suggestively along the sides of her waist, inches from the swell of her breasts. A breathing space was forgotten, her own hands moving to intercept his, frantically pushing them away from his objective.

"You don't like that?" he murmured. A hand left her waist to move to the back of her head. "I don't suppose you like it when a man runs his fingers though your hair, either."

This time he didn't allow her to deter him from his objective. The tortoise-shell clasp was unsnapped and tossed to the floor. He raked his fingers through the silken fire of her hair, sending it cascading around her shoulders and neck like molten lava.

Its release removed the valve of her temper. No matter how useless it might be, Lara struggled, twisting and turning, trying to elude his exploring hands. All the while his silent laughter mocked her efforts. Finally she started to bring her knee up, but he blocked her attack by knocking her other leg from beneath her. She fell heavily against him, momentarily knocking him off balance.

In that split second she twisted free.

CHAPTER SIX

BREATHING HEAVILY, Lara backed away warily. Rans was between her and the door. With the swiftness of his reflexes, there wasn't a chance that she could run by him and escape. He made no move toward her, standing there with his hands resting on his hips, dimples carved by the arrogant smile, brown eyes glittering brightly as they swept knowingly over her.

Rumpled red gold hair fell loosely around her shoulders in alluring disarray. The top two buttons of her blouse had come undone during the struggle, gaping the front to reveal the curving swell of her breasts, rising and falling in agitated breathing.

The composed mask was gone from her face. A becoming pink shade rouged her cheekbones. Her widened eyes were a turbulent green, guardedly alert to the slightest movement by Rans. Nervously Lara moistened her lips, which had become dry with fear.

"Get out of here." Her voice quivered and Rans laughed lowly at the weakness of her command.

A retreating foot nudged an object behind her. Lara knew she must be close to the stable wall. She let her gaze leave Rans for the split second it took to glance over her shoulder. A pitchfork was leaning against the wall. Before the thought was formed in her mind, she was grabbing it, pointing the pronged ends at Rans.

"Get out of here," she ordered, more certain now with a weapon in her hands that she was able to defend herself.

The amusement faded from his smile, although the smiling expression remained on his rough features. His eyes narrowed with measuring thoughtfulness. There was a faint tensing of his previously relaxed and mocking attitude.

With a flash of intuition, Lara realized she had made a mistake. Rans had never intended to try to recapture her as she had feared. If he had, he would have done it already. No, he had only been playing with her like a satiated cat plays with a trapped mouse for the fun of it, then walks away, letting the mouse go free for another day's game.

Lara wavered. Brandishing the pitchfork had changed the game, but it was too late to put it down now. The threat was made and she had to follow through with it, or cower submissively at his feet. That she would never do.

His hands moved from his hips, alert and ready for battle. With slow purposeful strides, Rans walked toward her, narrowing the gap between himself and the pointed ends of the pitchfork. She tried to swallow away the tightness in her throat.

"Stay away from me," Lara warned, tipping her head slightly to the side as she raised the pitchfork a fraction of an inch.

Rans didn't alter his stride, stopping only when the pointed ends of the pitchfork were pricking the front of his shirt. Nervously her fingers clenched and unclenched the handle. Courage deserted her at the blatant way he was ignoring her threat.

"Don't you want to run the pitchfork through me?" he taunted, his gaze boring into her troubled green eyes. "A woman is entitled to defend her honor."

"Leave me alone," Lara murmured desperately.

The tips wavered as if the weight of the pitchfork had become too heavy. Before she could steady her shaking arms, his hand had sliced upward, gripped the handle just in front of the prongs and shoved it away from his chest. Lara forgot to let go of her end and his twisting, pulling motion drew her within his reach as he yanked the weapon from her hands.

The bay whinnied nervously in his stall, the uneasy shifting of metal clad hooves echoing loudly in the stable. The hammering of Lara's frightened heart drowned out even that as she kicked and clawed at her captor, emitting the gasping, distress cries of a trapped animal.

An iron band circled her waist, lifting her feet

off the floor. Her fists flailed at his head and he turned her in his arms so she had no target. The heel of her shoe found his shinbone. His grip loosened and her feet touched the ground. Lara nearly spun out of his hold for the second time.

Instead she went crashing onto the floor, her fall broken by the cushioning mound of hay. Rans was there immediately, the weight of his body holding her down while he seized her wrists and stretched her arms above her head.

"Let me go!" she cried in angry frustration, glaring at the hewn face above her own.

"Not a chance, hellcat," Rans chuckled. "Not until you've learned your lesson."

The smoldering light in his eyes warned her of his intentions. Frantically she twisted her face into her arm to elude the satirical mouth moving toward her. Holding her slender wrists with one hand, steel fingers of his free hand wrenched her chin around, subjecting Lara to the punishment of his hard mouth.

There was no escape from the smothering pressure that ground her lips against her teeth. Her body writhed beneath his pinning length, crushed by his weight until she could hardly breathe. Blackness swirled behind her closed eyes as her lungs were deprived of oxygen. The strength to resist and struggle ebbed to nothing.

The cruelty of his kiss eased at her submission. Lara noted the change with relief as Rans seemed to breathe life into her instead of stealing it away.

His fingers left her chin to tangle themselves in the silken mass of her flame-colored hair.

His lips moved over the skin his grip had bruised. No longer suffocated by his mouth, Lara gulped in shaky breaths, inhaling his musky scent at the same time. Absently she was aware of his mouth moving along her jaw, pausing to nibble the lobe of her ear, then trailing down the sensitive nerves of her neck.

The hay scratched at her arms. Lara made a protesting movement against it and her wrists were released. Slowly she drew her arms down, and blood surged into the numbed limbs. As the ability to feel returned, she became conscious of the seductive quality in his touch. Her skin was tingling where Rans was lightly nibbling on her neck.

"No," Lara breathed. Her hands moved to strain against his muscular chest.

As if obeying, his mouth left her neck only to close sensuously over her lips. She realized then that he didn't intend to let her go until she responded. Her heartbeat quickened in fear. Instantly his hand began caressing her shoulder and neck in the most soothing manner, easing the rigid tension the thought had evoked.

"Relax," Rans murmured huskily against the corner of her lips.

Seemingly minus a will of her own, Lara obeyed. His mouth opened moistly over hers, reminding her how to kiss with passion, an art she thought she had forgotten until his expertise recalled it. The intimate exploration of the kiss aroused desires she had believed long dead.

The wildfire shooting through her veins melted what little cold resistance that remained. A leaping pulse hastened the thaw. The wonder of his touch filled Lara with awe. A million new sensations seemed to be splintering through her.

Her hand inched closer to the curling thickness of the hair on his neck. His own fingers loosened themselves from the silken tangle of her hair, trailing evocatively down her neck to the hollow of her throat.

A sighing moan of shuddering surrender came from her throat when his fingers released the buttons of her blouse. Her breast swelled to the cup of his hand. Lara slid her hand inside his shirt, reveling in the burning nakedness of his skin. What was happening to her was crazy, crazy and glorious.

A whirlpool of emotion had her spinning. The warm moistness of his lips trailed languidly down her neck to kiss the rounded curve of her breast while his hand moved along her hip, molding her pliant flesh against his hard length. Senses vibrated with secret longings. Of its own volition, her body moved suggestively against his.

His head raised to claim her mouth again, tasting the hunger of her parted lips, the kiss deepening with elemental desire. A radiant glow of ecstasy filled Lara's heart with a joy beyond expression. The abandoned fervidness of her response was her way of sharing the profound emotion awakening within her.

There was a withdrawal of his lips from hers. Lara waited to feel the fiery trail touch her again. Rans's weight shifted slightly away from her. The red gold tips of her lashes fluttered upward, an expectant glow in her green eyes, the ardent fire veiled by her lashes.

Rans was watching her, a mysteriously hard light in his eyes. The cynical curve of his mouth was formed neither by amusement nor contentment. A chill ran down her spine, its icy fingers a warning.

"You are full of surprises, aren't you, Mrs. Cochran?" he murmured, drawing a deep, calming breath. "Maybe I should let your husband in on your little secret."

"Wh-what secret?" Lara whispered shakily.

What did he mean? Was he going to tell Trevor what he'd done? The way he'd kissed her and she had kissed back? Why? For what possible purpose? To hurt her?

"That all it takes is a little brute force to change you from a frigid wildcat to a sex kitten," Rans mocked.

Scarlet stained her cheeks as waves of unbearable heat swept through her. Swiftly Lara rolled from beneath him, sitting up with her legs curled beneath her in the hay, her back turned to him, her head bent in almost unendurable shame.

"That's not true," she protested in a choked

voice. Her fingers fumbled with the buttons of her blouse, fastening only two when the hay rustled beside her.

"Isn't it?" Rans turned her partially around, his hand sliding under her blouse onto her ribs. "Shall I prove it?"

Her head remained downcast, the fiery curtain of her hair concealing her expression from his probing gaze. Tears of shame burned her eyes as Lara silently acknowledged the power Rans seemed to have over her flesh. Even if she struggled, she knew she would be ultimately overpowered by the potent force of his masculinity.

In her heart she knew it would only be a token struggle. The rapture she had felt at his caress was still too fresh in her mind. There was no need for him to prove her susceptibility to his lovemaking.

"Don't." A trembling whisper as weak and shaky as her limbs from the desire he had awakened. "Please," she added, asking for his mercy.

Her heart hammered wildly as he withdrew his hand from her bare skin, then crooked a forefinger under her chin to raise it. White teeth were holding her quivering lower lip still. At his continued lack of movement and silence, Lara lifted her lashes to gaze imploringly at him. One crystal teardrop hovered on the tip of a lash.

The unreadable depths of his brown eyes held her attention while a finger touched the lash holding the tear. It slipped onto his fingers.

"You wanted to make love to me, didn't you?" Rans stated, his chiseled expression revealing nothing, not even the effects of the lust-filled moments they had shared.

"Yes. Yes. *Yes*!" Her voice rising in a crescendo of hurt and humiliation, ending with a cymbal crashing, "I hate you!"

He seemed to find her vehemence amusing. He studied the movement of his thumb as it rubbed the wetness of her tear on his finger. With animal litheness, he rolled to his feet, towering above her while Lara glared at him, her head thrown back proudly.

"Poor Mrs. Cochran," he said with cutting laughter in his voice. "You are human, after all."

Her eyes filled with tears, as if somewhere a dam had burst. Blinded by the flood, Lara didn't see Rans leave. She only heard the closing of the stable door. Salty tears ran down her cheeks, their briny taste coating her lips.

It was nearly half an hour before she had sufficient control of herself to sneak back into the house. In the privacy of her room it started all over again. She had once sworn that she would never let a man hurt her again, but she had never expected to meet anyone like Rans MacQuade.

The next morning Lara had to force herself to go downstairs to join her father and Trevor at the breakfast table. She was certain they would notice the change in her. The shell that had protected her was gone. She was a vulnerable woman again. Neither of them—and not even Sara, who knew her so well—appeared to see any difference in her. She felt temporarily safe for a little while longer.

But the moment she dreaded most of all had not yet occurred. She still had to meet Rans face to face. The more days that went by without it happening, the more she dreaded the confrontation. Would pride keep her composed or would she dissolve like a bowl of gelatin at the sight of him, remembering the way she had humiliated herself in his arms?

When the moment came, Lara still wasn't prepared for it. She and Sara had finished the evening dishes and Lara was on her way to her room, intending to hide there behind the pages of a book. As she crossed the entry hall to the staircase, the study door opened and her father stepped out.

"Lara, are you busy?" Martin Alexander halted just outside the opened door.

She hesitated, then turned away from the stairs to walk toward her father. "Not particularly. Why?"

"Would you bring a pot of coffee into the study?" he asked. "Rans and I are discussing the chapter outlines of my book."

Her gaze flew past him through the open door, riveting on the man in the chair facing the desk. The study light gleamed over the dark golden brown of his hair. Her pulse leaped and there was a crazy singing in her ears. For an instant Lara was afraid she would faint, then she regained control of her senses.

"Of course, I will, daddy," she agreed, planning to deputize Sara to bring the pot.

"And bring three cups," he instructed.

"Three?" she frowned.

"Yes, I want you to join us."

Lara swallowed, smiling nervously. "Another time, maybe. There were, uh, some things I wanted to get done tonight."

He waved the protest aside. "Let them wait."

"But you will be talking about the book, technical things—"

"Exactly," Martin nodded. "Rans seems to think I should have separate chapters on disease and insects, because— Well, never mind. We'll go into the reasons later, but I want your opinion too." The matter was settled as far as he was concerned and he turned to reenter the study, pausing to add, "You might bring some of Sara's pecan tarts with the coffee."

Then he was inside, closing the door. Lara was left standing there, her mind still racing to find a suitable excuse to refuse. She stared at the door for a long second before deciding that she was foolish to prolong this meeting. It was best to get it over with.

Wings from a million butterflies fluttered madly in her stomach as she walked to the kitchen. Her throat was dry and tight, with hardly enough moisture in her mouth to swallow. She poured the coffee into the Thermos server and set it on the tray with the cups and saucers, adding a plate of Sara's tarts.

At the study door, Lara took a deep breath to steady her jumping nerves, balanced the tray on one hand and opened the door. As she walked in, her gaze was magnetically drawn to Rans, sliding away when he politely rose at her entrance.

"Here's your coffee and sweet, daddy." She walked to the second leather chair in front of the desk, setting the tray atop the cleared space on the desk. Her glance ricocheted off Rans's carved features. "Good evening, Mr. MacQuade."

"Mrs. Cochran." He acknowledged her greeting smoothly.

He continued to stand, setting off the butterflies again in her stomach with the way he towered muscularly beside her. "Please sit down," Lara insisted with a forced smile.

Another glance in his direction was caught by his brown eyes. He appeared aloof and remarkably indifferent to her, as if the incident in the stable had happened to two other people. Nothing in his expression revealed even a hint of taunting mockery.

A little sigh of relief quivered through her as she turned to her father. "Would you like me to pour, daddy?"

"Please." He looked up from the notes in his hand. "Do you take anything in your coffee, Rans? Sugar? Cream? Honey?"

"Nothing, thank you."

There was only a slight trembling of her hand as Lara poured the coffee into the three cups, adding honey to her father's and setting it to the right of him. The cup for Rans jiggled in its saucer when she picked it up to hand it to him.

His tanned fingers were reaching out for it, but his attention was diverted by her father bringing up some point about his book. Lara didn't hear it. She was too busy concentrating on maintaining her composure.

As his hand closed over the saucer, it accidentally came in contact with Lara's. An electric current seemed to spring from his touch, jolting her so that she jerked her fingers back. Her action was not swift enough to elude the cup of coffee as it tipped, spilling its nearly boiling contents on the back of her hand.

The clatter of the cup in its china saucer and Lara's stifled cry of pain instantly had both men's attention. She was gripping her wrist, the fingers of her injured hand spread. Her skin was already turning a fiery red from the scalding liquid.

"What happened?" her father said dimly.

Rans was already on his feet, the emptied cup shoved on the desk. "She's burned her hand with the coffee." An inner instinct had backed Lara away from him, but she was too numbed by the pain to increase the distance when Rans moved toward her. "We'd better get some cold water on it right away."

His hand was under her elbow, guiding her

from the room, taking charge of the situation before Lara could protest. "It's n-not serious." Her teeth were slightly clenched from the pain. "I can take care of it myself. Really."

But he was already opening the door to the bathroom on the ground floor and escorting her inside. The cold-water faucet in the sink was turned on and her injured hand unceremoniously thrust into the water.

"Is there any salve around to put on it?" Rans inquired briskly.

He was standing so close beside her that Lara could feel the heat of his body. Disturbed by his nearness, she moved to the side of the sink, keeping her head down and her gaze on her hand beneath the running water.

"There should be some in the medicine cabinet behind the sink mirror. On the second shelf, I think." She swallowed, her heart beating like a thousand snare drums. She tried once more to reject his aid. "There's no need for you to stay. I can take care of it."

Her statement was ignored as he opened the mirrored door above the sink. He found the tube of salve immediately, removing it from the shelf and closing the door. Lara could feel his gaze studying her and hoped her profile didn't reveal the tension that strained her poise.

"Does it feel better?" he asked after another minute had passed with cooling water running over her hand.

"Yes, it . . . it doesn't burn anymore." The brief shake of her head was designed to flip the hair away from her face, a self-conscious movement since her red gold hair was securely pinned in an impeccable coil.

Rans turned off the faucet and reached for the towel hanging in the ringed rack. He ignored her outstretched hand to take it from him and gently wrapped the soft towel around her other hand. Carefully he pressed the towel against injured skin to absorb the moisture.

With his attention diverted to her hand, Lara allowed herself to glance at his face. The strong lines were so aggressively masculine, sun browned and rugged. Thick and spiky lashes, not femininely long and curling like Trevor's, veiled the brown of his piercing eyes, a velvet shade to conceal the steel of his gaze. There was a hardness to his mouth, faintly cynical and faintly ruthless. She remembered its mastery when it had taken intimate possession of hers.

The memory stirred the physical longings within her, and Lara hastily glanced away from his mouth. Instead she concentrated on the drying motion of his hands. They were large and powerful like their owner, yet capable of gentleness as well as bruising force. Her breasts tingled with the memory of the erotic caress of those hands. Lara breathed in sharply at how vividly she recalled the sensation.

Instantly his gaze narrowed on her face. "Does it still bother you?"

For a startled second, she thought he had read her mind, blushing self-consciously when she realized he was referring to the burn on her hand.

"No, it hardly hurts at all." Which was not exactly true since her hand was still uncomfortably tender. "I was thinking about something else."

His mouth quirked with amusement as Rans darted her a glittering look. "Something else that makes you gasp with pain?" he mocked, unwrapping the towel from her hand.

Lara hesitated, unwilling to answer what amounted to a leading question. "I didn't gasp." She reached for the tube of salve. "I'll put it on."

"I'll do it. It'll be faster," Rans rejected her offer, then resumed the former subject. "If it wasn't a gasp, what was it?"

His fingers began to rub the cream onto the faint pink area of her hand, his gentle touch nearly as soothing as the burn ointment. Her throat ached and Lara couldn't answer his question. The rhythmic massage of his fingers was making her weak. Finally she knew her poise would splinter if she had to endure it any longer, so she yanked her hand away.

"That's good enough. It's much better now, thank you," she said stiffly. Her eyes bounced away from the quizzical arch of his brow.

"You look a little pale. Are you sure you're all right?" he questioned.

Lara wavered. The close quarters of the bathroom would not let her get to the door without brushing past him. At this moment she needed to avoid any contact. As much as she claimed to despise him because of his cynical mockery, she was disturbingly attracted to him physically.

Rans misunderstood the reason for her silence. When her lashes fluttered in silent frustration, he reached out to steady her. Flinching from his hand, Lara took a step backward.

"Leave me alone, please." It was a breathless order.

Their eyes locked. A hard, knowing light slowly glittered in his gaze. A cold smile cruelly curved his mouth as he looked deeply into her eyes, reading the fear that she tried to conceal.

"I assure you, Mrs. Cochran, I had no intention of doing otherwise." Rans jeered cynically.

His words chilled her. Lara tried to tell herself she was glad that she didn't interest him in a physical way, that it was what she wanted to hear. She didn't want him to touch her again or hold her in his arms. She wanted to forget the incident had ever happened.

"Good," she said shortly. "I'm glad."

"Not that I didn't enjoy our little romp in the hay the other night." His husky voice laughed at the prim tilt of her chin.

"I don't wish to discuss that offensive incident." Lara broke away from his mocking gaze.

"Has your husband discovered the breach in your marble facade?" His gaze roamed over her with suggestive laziness.

"My private life is none of your business!" she retorted sharply.

Rans chuckled. "Maybe I should give him a few lessons on how to make you purr instead of spit."

"You are despicable and disgusting! If you were a gentleman, you would have the good manners not to bring up the subject!" Her eyes flashed with green sparks. "I loathe the sight of you!"

"I'm not a gentleman. And you are not a lady—" his gaze flicked down to her hands "—or your fingers wouldn't be curling with the urge to claw my eyes out like a common alleycat. Believe me," Rans continued with a harsh grin, "the dislike is mutual. I don't think much of a woman who uses sex as a weapon to bring her husband to heel. Especially when she becomes cold and bitter because the attempt backfired in her face."

Instinctively her hand swung in an arc, the palm stinging against his cheek. With his reflexes, he could have eluded her hand, but he hadn't blinked an eye. Lara faced him, trembling with the rage of her temper from his erroneous insult.

"Do you feel better?" Rans taunted softly.

" Yes!" Lara hissed.

"Then shall we call it even?"

She was wary. "Why?"

"You live here and I work here. That makes it inevitable that we'll run into each other again. I can learn to tolerate you if we don't keep crossing swords every time we meet," he concluded.

"Tolerate me?" Lara gasped. He was the one

who had come and disrupted everything. She hadn't been happy exactly, but she hadn't been discontented with her life, either. Now she wasn't certain that the same thing would hold true. "You are insufferably arrogant."

"And you are an insensitive bitch." Dimples were carved in his lean cheeks. "Are we going to continue to trade insults or shall we make a pact of peaceful coexistence?"

Fuming inwardly, she held her silence for several seconds before she grudgingly agreed. "A pact."

There was a mockingly arrogant inclination of his head. "Good. Shall we return to the study before your father decides that you seriously burned your hand?"

"You go ahead," Lara refused tightly. "Make my excuses. I'm sure you can come up with something that's convincing."

After letting Rans have a head start, Lara hurried up the stairs to her room. The pact would never work. Whenever Rans MacQuade was around, her reaction to him was inevitably warlike . . . or loverlike, a small voice added.

CHAPTER SEVEN

THE LEATHER REINS were looped around as Lara walked between the row of trees. The branches arched above her head, covered with new leaves of a bright spring green. The bay hunter blew softly against her shoulder. Lara paused to stroke its velvet nose.

A tear slid down her cheek, tickling the corner of her mouth. Impatiently she brushed it away, wondering where it had come from. It was spring. The pecan trees were bursting with life. She should feel happy, instead of trapped in this melancholy mood.

Not even Angie's letter in the morning mail had cheered her up as it usually did. Instead her friendly prattle about her husband, Bob, and the redecoration of their house had struck a sad chord. Angie's letter had been no different from others Lara had received from her, but Lara was different.

Once she had found contentment in the emptiness of her marriage. She had honestly believed her life to be fulfilling. She had even boasted to

Angie that it was everything she wanted. Now she wondered.

A pickup truck drove past the orchard, stirring up dust. Lara recognized it as the one Rans always drove before she heard the brakes being applied. Quickly she scrubbed her cheeks, to be certain there was no trace of tears.

A slam of the truck door confirmed that he had stopped. Within seconds Lara saw him vaulting the white fence and walking toward her. Surprisingly, their tentative pact had worked thus far. It had only been tested in meetings that had included her father.

She couldn't begin to guess why he was stopping to see her now. He was definitely not someone she wanted to see at this particular moment when her spirits were so downcast.

"Hello!" he called. "Problems?"

Lara shook her head. "No." Her hand continued to stroke the blazed face of the bay, avoiding the directness of Rans's gaze when he reached them.

"I thought your horse might have gone lame again. That's why I stopped," Rans explained.

"He's fine. Fully recovered," she assured him. "I was just cooling him off before we got back to the stable." She could feel the piercing examination of his eyes and wished the pact was not in force. She didn't feel like being polite to him. "I'm sorry you were delayed without cause."

"You've been crying. Is something wrong?" he observed quietly.

"You're mistaken." A hand moved defensively to her face.

"Your mascara is smudged."

Lara ran a quick finger beneath the lower lash of each eye, a telltale dark brown staining her finger. "Perspiration," she lied. "We galloped nearly all the way here."

"Really?" Rans mocked her excuse. "That's also why your eyes are red and swollen, too, I suppose."

"I'm tired and in no mood to match words with you." Irritation flashed through her at his damnable perception. She gathered up the horse's reins and looped them over its head. "It's time I was getting back to the house."

"The No Trespassing message came through loud and clear," he replied dryly, stepping to the horse's head and taking hold of the bridle.

"Good."

Her coordination was jerky as Lara gripped the reins along the hunter's neck and held the stirrup to mount. When she started to swing into the saddle, her boot slipped off the metal stirrup, sending her down. She stumbled and would have fallen to the ground if Rans's long length hadn't been there to check her fall.

Her flesh melted at the searing contact with his masculine form. The bay's hindquarters swung away from the pair while Rans's grip immediately

tightened around her waist. He was so strong and
she was so weak. Lara wanted to lean against him
and absorb some of his strength.

For a few seconds she allowed herself to do
that. Her head rested against his chest, listening to
the rapid and strong beat of his heart, and feeling
the warmth of his breath near her skin. The
brushing touch of his mouth against her hair trig-
gered an awareness of what she was doing. Her
defenses had crumbled to the point where she was
inviting his caress.

Her hands stiffened against the rippling muscles
in his arms as Lara pushed herself from the disturbing warmth of his body. She stared at a button
on his shirt. His grip loosened, making no attempt
to check her withdrawal.

"I'm sorry." Lara wasn't certain why she was
apologizing to him. Maybe the words were really
spoken for herself. "I was more tired than I realized."

"Let me give you a leg up." His voice was tautly
controlled.

"Thank you," she murmured, feeling choked
by a sudden surge of emotion.

The bay was swung back into position. His large
hand was offered palm upward for her boot. Ef-
fortlessly Lara was boosted into the saddle. She
had lacked the courage to look at Rans until she
was safely removed from his nearness.

The enigmatic light in his brown eyes held her
captive, her heartbeat skipping erratically all over

the place. His left hand held the reins while his right rested on her knee. An empty ache started devouring her insides.

"I have to go," Lara murmured desperately as if he was asking her to stay.

"Tell your father I'll stop by with the quarterly reports tonight." Rans stepped away. He seemed suddenly very aloof and indifferent.

"Yes. Yes, I will," she answered tightly, reining the horse away from him as scalding tears welled in her green eyes.

Lara barely remembered any of the ride to the house. She simply gave the bay hunter his head and let him take her back. Trevor was on his way out when she rounded the corner of the house.

He paused to wait for her. "I'm glad I saw you before I left," he said. "I left a note in the kitchen to let Sara know I wouldn't be here for dinner this evening. Knowing her, she is liable to throw it away thinking it's a scrap of waste paper. So would you pass the message on to her to be safe?"

"Yes," she agreed automatically. "Where will you be?"

A raven brow lifted with cynical dryness. "Do you care?" Trevor jeered.

Lara sighed and ran a weary hand over her forehead. "No." she started to walk past him to the front door, but he caught her arm.

"You seem different," he frowned curiously. "I can't put my finger on why."

His touch made her skin crawl. "You are mistaken, Trevor," she said with freezing scorn.

"Am I?" His dark head tipped to the side in considering thoughtfulness. "I'm not sure."

"Don't you have some place you have to be?" Lara snapped, not wanted to be subjected to his probing for fear of what he might discover... or what she might discover about herself.

His dark eyes flicked impatiently to his watch. "Yes, I'm late now. We'll talk another time, Lara."

Not if she could help it, she thought as he released her arm and walked swiftly to his car parked in the driveway. Lara didn't wait to see him leave, but hurried into the house, rubbing her arm where he had touched her.

The courtyard was darkened by evening shadows. Lara turned away from the glass-paned door, twirling the liquor in her glass and listening to the clink of ice against the sides. She ran a nervous hand along the waistband of her long skirt, a vivid floral pattern against a background of black.

After the quiet meal shared with her father, Lara had not wanted her own company. To be alone meant to think. That was one thing she didn't want to do. So she had accompanied her father to his study, sharing an after-dinner drink with him, breaking her usual custom of abstinence.

But his company hadn't proved to be the distraction she had hoped. Soon after they had entered the study, Martin Alexander had become immersed in the notes she had typed for him today, leaving Lara to restlessly wander about the room.

"What time is it?" he asked with a frowning glance from his papers.

Looking at the delicate gold oval of her wristwatch, she answered, "Nearly half past eight." How could time go by so slowly?

His mouth straightened with grim impatience. "That mechanic said he'd have my car out here by no later than eight o'clock. I shouldn't have left it with him. I could have waited to have the oil changed and the tires rotated another time when I wouldn't be needing it the next day."

"I'm sure he'll be here if he said he would bring it tonight," Lara assured him absently.

"I hope so or—" His sentence was interrupted by a knock at the front door. "Maybe he's finally here," he grumbled, rising from his desk to answer the door.

Taking one of the books from the shelf, Lara flipped through it disinterestedly and slid it back in its place. With a dispirited sigh, she wandered to the red brick fireplace. Through the open study door, she heard the voices in the entry hall and stiffened.

"Rans. Come in," Martin instructed in a surprised and pleased tone. "I didn't expect to see you tonight."

"I mentioned to your daughter this morning that I would be bringing the quarterly reports to you."

"It probably slipped her mind," was the dismissing reply. "Come into the study."

In a flash of honesty, Lara realized that everything had been a lie. It had not been a mere whim that had prompted her to wear the decidedly flattering outfit of a black chiffon blouse and complementing flowered skirt. Nor had it been a desire for a change that had led her to style her hair to flow freely down her back, gold combs holding it away from her face.

She hadn't joined her father in his study because she hadn't wanted the solitude of her own company or because she had wanted the companionship of his. Subconsciously she had plotted her actions, arranging circumstances so that she could see Rans MacQuade and hopefully have him notice her.

The discovery panicked Lara. Even the drink in her hand had been calculated in a weak attempt to gain courage. She wanted to run but it was already too late. Footsteps were approaching the door. Quickly she swallowed the remainder of her drink, but her legs were shaking when she turned toward the door.

"Good evening, Mr. MacQuade." A stiffly polite smile curved her mouth as he stepped into the room, tall and vital and compellingly attractive. "I'm afraid I didn't pass on your message to daddy. I forgot all about running into you this morning while I was riding." A half-truth since she had forgot the message but not their meeting.

"No harm done." Rans shrugged, running an impersonal eye over the length of her.

"How about a drink, Rans?" Martin Alexander inquired. "A whiskey, maybe?"

"Sounds fine."

As her father started toward the built-in bar near the door, there was another knock on the front door. He glanced at his daughter.

"Maybe that's the mechanic." He shook his head, not holding out much hope. "Do you want to help yourself, Rans, while I answer the door? Lara can show you where things are if you can't find what you want."

But Rans didn't require her assistance as he stepped behind the bar. She covertly watched him dump several cubes of ice in a squat glass and pour a shot of whiskey from the bottle beneath the counter over the ice.

He glanced at the empty glass in her hand. "Would you like another?"

"Please." She carried her glass to the bar for him to refill. "A Bacardi cocktail. Sweet."

A few minutes later he handed the glass back. "How's that?"

Lara sipped it experimentally. "Perfect," she smiled nervously, clutching the glass in her trembling hands. "I shall have to remember your talent."

His mouth quirked in dry amusement. At that moment her father reentered the room, smiling in a slightly harried fashion.

"The mechanic is here with my car," he announced. "I have to drive him back to town. Can you stay for a few minutes, Rans? I'd like to go over these reports with you since you're here. I shouldn't be gone long.''

"I can stay for a while," Rans agreed.

"Good." Martin Alexander nodded. "Lara can keep you entertained while I'm gone."

With that, he left the room. Lara had seen the glittering mockery that had been in Rans's gaze at her father's last remark. His attitude didn't lessen the tension that scraped at her raw nerves.

The silence was beginning to build in the room. Rans walked leisurely to the fireplace, resting a foot on the raised hearth and leaning an arm against the mantel. He appeared relaxed while Lara was as taut as a violin string.

"There was something else I forgot to mention this morning." She tried to sound nonchalant as she wandered to a chair near the fireplace, standing behind it as if it offered protection.

"What's that?" He slid her a lazy glance.

Lara had difficulty meeting it, feeling guilty because her reasons for being in the room were less than honorable. "My father's birthday is a week from Saturday. We are having a small dinner party for him in town to celebrate. I know he would like you to be there if you're free that evening."

"I have nothing planned."

"Good. I'll count on you to be there, then," Lara replied with stiff politeness. "Of course, you are welcome to bring a friend." It was an attempt to deny that Rans had the power to attract her. "You do have a girl friend?"

"I have someone I can invite if you are sure you don't mind." His dark head was tipped to the side in inquiry.

The words stabbed. "Why should I mind?" She forced a careless shrug. "It's perfectly all right with me if you bring someone." She took a bolstering sip of her drink and looked away. "I wasn't certain if you were seeing anyone, but I thought I should suggest that you were free to bring a partner for the evening."

"You are not the only one with a private life, Mrs. Cochran," Rans mocked.

Lara flinched at his cutting tone but refused to let the conversation turn into an exchange of insults. "Is she from Hattiesburg?"

"Yes."

"Have you known her long . . . or is that too personal?"

A faint bitterness crept into her voice.

"It is personal, but I don't mind answering it," he replied evenly. "I met her shortly after I came to work here."

"Really. Obviously you like her or you wouldn't still be seeing her." Lara stared at the pink liquid of her drink, fighting the constriction that gripped her throat. She tossed her head back in a gesture of uncaring pride.

"That's right."

"What does she do . . . for a living, I mean?" she faltered.

"She has a respectable profession, if that's what you're asking." Sardonic dimples appeared in his tanned cheeks. "She's a nurse."

"I didn't mean to imply anything of the kind," she laughed hollowly trying to make a joke out of his sarcastic remark.

The liquor didn't seem to be able to settle her quivering nerves. Lara reached for a cigarette case on the round table beside the chair. Her shaking fingers couldn't make the cigarette lighter work properly. Rans was there, taking it out of her hand and snapping the flame to the tip of her cigarette.

"Ann is twenty-six, divorced and has a four-year-old boy," Rans continued. "She's taller than you with blond hair and blue eyes, attractive in a quiet, gentle way. Would you like her vital statistics?"

"No." Hurt flashed in her eyes, and Lara quickly veiled it with her lashes.

She inhaled nervously on the cigarette, studying the red imprint of her lipstick on the filtered tip. He was standing much too close. Out of the corner of her eye she could see the dark hairs on his chest curling above the unbuttoned collar of his shirt.

"Where is Trevor tonight?" He reversed the roles and became the inquisitor.

"I don't know." The red gold curls danced between her shoulder blades as she shook her head.

"Did you ask where he was going?" he mocked.

"Yes, I did, but he didn't tell me." She lifted her chin proudly. "If he had, it would probably have been a lie, anyway."

"Why do you say that?" The hard brown eyes subjected her to a measured look.

"Because Trevor doesn't know how to tell the truth." A resigned, bitterly amused sigh accompanied the exhaled smoke. "'Men are deceivers ever,'" Lara quoted a line she had once heard, the author forgotten.

"That's a cynical remark from one so young and beautiful," Rans observed dryly.

"It's the truth." Her eyes challenged him to deny it. "I know you will find this hard to believe, but I was once a very happy bride. Of course the happiness barely lasted past the honeymoon. Prince Charming turned out to be Prince Chaser."

An eyebrow was raised in preoccupied thought as Rans studied the ice in his glass. Then his narrowed gaze swept to the marble facade of her expression with disconcerting appraisal.

"So you've sworn off all men," he said quietly.

A tiredness rushed through her. She was tired of being alone, of constantly holding herself aloof. She wanted to be touched, to be caressed, to be the object of someone's affections. She wanted to be needed and cared for and to lean on someone else instead of always being apart. She wanted to share her joy and her sorrow with someone. Before she could give in to that tide of weakness, Lara walked slowly to the fireplace.

"At least, I won't be disillusioned anymore," she returned.

"You haven't stopped being disillusioned, Mrs. Cochran."

"There isn't any point in being formal considering how personal our conversation has become." She smiled wryly, glancing at him. "Please call me Lara."

His compelling gaze refused to let her look away. "I think not." Rans drained his glass, a grimness in the line of his mouth.

"Why?" Lara breathed, her heart pounding almost louder than her voice.

"Because I prefer to remind myself that you are married." Rans slid her another raking glance.

A paralysis seemed to claim her limbs, making movement of any kind impossible. She wanted to read more into his words and knew she didn't dare. The air was suddenly crackling with high-voltage tension. Rans snapped the connection by walking to the bar and setting his glass on the counter.

"When Martin returns, explain that I wasn't able to stay any longer," he said curtly. "Good night, Mrs. Cochran."

His exit from the study left Lara with the sensation that he had taken some part of her with him. It frightened her. Everything that had happened that night frightened her with its implications. She had arranged to see him. She had arranged that he notice her. She had directed the conversation to a personal level. Now Lara wanted to elude the knowledge of what that meant.

As the hour of her father's birthday dinner drew closer, Lara wished she could cancel it. Of course it was impossible. All the arrangements had been made, and the guests on their way.

Lara pressed a hand to her throbbing temple, knowing an excuse of a headache would be true. There were two reasons why she couldn't use it. A glance at the dark-haired man behind the wheel of the car found one of the reasons. If Trevor attended the dinner without her, the gossip about their marriage would increase to the point where it would become difficult to hold her head up among their friends and acquaintances.

The second reason was that she had to conquer her physical emotions where Rans was concerned. She couldn't spend the rest of her life cowardly avoiding him. No matter how much pain it caused, it was best that she attend the dinner tonight and see him with another woman. That's all it had taken to kill her feelings for Trevor.

"Do you suppose there is anything going on between Martin and Charlotte Thompson?" Trevor mused absently, breaking the silence as they entered the city limits of Hattiesburg.

Charlotte Thompson was the widow of Clayton Thompson, who had been one of her father's oldest and dearest friends. He had decided to escort her to the dinner tonight rather than have her come alone.

"I doubt if it was more than a friendly gesture," Lara replied indifferently.

Trevor chuckled softly. "My dear, your father isn't so old that he wouldn't enjoy some feminine companionship."

"Is that all you ever think about?" Lara accused in a flash of irritation.

"Don't you *ever* think about it?" Trevor returned with biting quietness.

Yes, she could have told him, much too often lately. And the desires were aroused by the wrong man. Instead Lara let his question slide past unanswered.

The other couples had just begun to arrive when Lara and Trevor reached the private dining hall that they had reserved for the evening. Lara didn't see Rans and his date arrive. She turned and he was standing near the portable bar with a drink already in his hand, and one in the blonde's.

Her breath caught in her throat at the way Rans was smiling at the woman, his eyes crinkling at the corners and lean grooves dimpling the tanned cheeks. Lara had to admit the girl was attractive in a freshly scrubbed, vitally animated way. Her ash-blond hair was short, cut in a boyish style that was appealing. Her lips seemed permanently curved in a friendly smile.

A few seconds later, Rans looked up and met Lara's gaze. His expression seemed to harden without a perceptible change showing in his smile. Then his hand was gripping the woman's elbow, and he was guiding her across the room to where Lara stood with Trevor and a few other guests.

In a haze of pain, Lara survived the introduction, saying all the right things at the right times. Using Trevor as a shield, Lara directed as much attention as she could to him. She knew her husband well enough to recognize the symptoms of a budding interest in Rans's companion, Ann Koffman.

Gratefully, another couple approached to divert them from Rans and his blond nurse. Afterward Lara took care to avoid the area of the large room where he was, and Trevor, portraying the model husband, stayed at her side. It was impossible to ignore Rans's presence. He was the only one in the room who was alive to her. The rest of the guests could have been robots instead of people.

At the announcement of dinner, Trevor directed the seating arrangements, splitting up the couples—to keep the conversation lively at the table, he said. As hostess, Lara took the chair at the opposite end of the table from her father, relieved to see Rans seated beside him, although still very much within her line of vision.

Trevor was making a show of seating Mrs. Thompson on his right, closer to the middle of the table. The reasoning behind his seating arrangements became apparent when Lara noticed Ann Koffman sitting in the chair to Trevor's left. The fact was noted by Rans, whose keen glance strayed to Lara. She avoided it quickly.

The food tasted like chalky paste to Lara. She ate mechanically, adding a token comment now and then to the conversation around her. Silently she observed Trevor's discreet maneuverings, knowing she wasn't the only one interested in what was happening.

It was a subtle charm Trevor used, asking a few polite questions of the blonde without appearing to devote all of his attention to her. By the time the meal was over, Ann Koffman was talking to him quite animatedly, a victim of his magnetic spell even if she wasn't consciously aware of it. But Lara was and Rans had to be.

The tables were cleared swiftly of the dishes by efficient waiters. Just as quickly the tables were removed from the room, almost without the guests being aware of it. A small dance combo slipped into the room, played a few testing notes, then offered a rousing rendition of Happy Birthday.

Trevor was at her side to claim the waltz that followed, leading her onto the small dance floor after her father and Mrs. Thompson had made the initial circle. At least in his arms, Lara didn't have to keep up the pretense of conversation.

Which was a good thing, because when she saw Rans dancing with Ann pain gripped her throat in a stranglehold. The knowledge that she had no right to be jealous only increased her abject misery. Afraid she might have revealed some of her inner feelings in her expression, Lara glanced hesitantly at Trevor. His gaze thoughtfully on the same couple.

"Did MacQuade tell you much about Miss Koffman?" he inquired absently.

Her lips mouthed the word "no" as she shook her head briefly. Her smarting green eyes studied the seam of Trevor's sleeve. Lara was too engulfed by her own agony to truly be aware that her husband was questioning her about another woman.

"He didn't mention whether they were serious?"

"He only said he had been seeing her for some time." She forced her answer out. "You'll have to do your own investigating to find out more than that."

The sharpness of her tone drew his darkened gaze. "I was merely expressing a curiosity," Trevor smiled.

"Why do you bother to lie?" Lara sighed with cynical bitterness. "You know very well that you have marked her out for your next conquest, regardless of whatever is between her and Rans McQuade."

"Are you giving me your blessing?" There was definite amusement in his voice.

"Trevor, you may jump into a bottomless pit, for all I care what you do," she returned caustically.

"Always the solicitous wife," he mocked, "aren't you, Lara, my love?"

"Just as you are the devoted husband."

"Why do you stay married to me?" His dark gaze roved curiously over her strained features.

"Don't ask that question," Lara answered with taut control, "or I might find that I don't have any reason anymore." Her green eyes flashed astutely at him. "And you don't want a divorce, do you? It's so much more convenient to be married and have your affairs on the side. I make a convenient scapegoat, don't I? Especially when the girl begins to pall." She laughed bitterly. "I even provide you with an excellent opening. The poor misunderstood husband with a frigid wife at home. Oh, God, you make me sick, Trevor."

He was angry. Angry and a little bit uncertain that perhaps he had pushed her too far. His tight-lipped silence brought a measure of satisfaction to Lara, and the discovery that her reference to a divorce had not been an idle threat.

"Have you ever considered that I might be more of a husband if you were more of a wife?" he said finally.

"But I'm not interested in being more of a wife to you," she pointed out to him. "If I were, I would not look the other way when you carry on your flirtations right in front of me."

The song ended. As Lara turned out of Trevor's arms, she was facing Rans, his expression impassive as he met her startled look. Her gaze darted to the hand resting lightly and possessively along the blond-haired woman's waist. A stab of envy pierced her midsection, remembering the firm touch of those large hands.

She would have turned and walked away,

unable to bear the sight of the two of them together, if Trevor had not stepped forward.

"It's a good band, isn't it?" Trevor commented as the combo swung into a lively tune.

"Yes, it is," the blonde agreed enthusiastically, an added sparkle entering her blue eyes under the influence of Trevor's flashing smile.

"Lara doesn't care to dance to the faster songs. Would you like to dance, Ann? May I call you Ann?" Trevor tacked on with old-fashioned courtesy.

"Yes, please, call me Ann." Before she accepted his invitation, she glanced to Rans and received a curt nod of permission, accompanied by a smile to take away the abruptness of his action. "And I would like to dance, thank you. Rans claims not to know the new steps."

"You don't mind, do you, dear?" Trevor inclined his head toward Lara, a faint challenge in his dark eyes.

"No," she murmured.

The truth was she minded very much. She didn't want to be left alone with Rans. Her strained nerves were already raw and painfully sensitive to his presence. But a protest at this point was impossible, as Trevor very well knew.

Nervously Lara watched the two of them step onto the dance floor, one tall and darkly handsome and the other willowy slender and fair. Rans was aware of Trevor's reputation. A covert glance out of the corner of her eye noted the iron set of his jaw as he, too, watched the pair. She quickly eluded his gaze when he suddenly glanced at her, his brown eyes narrowing.

"You look in need of a drink. May I get you one?" Rans offered in a slightly forbidding tone.

"Please," she replied, grateful for any distraction, however brief.

CHAPTER EIGHT

WITHIN A FEW MINUTES Rans was back. "A Bacardi cocktail, sweet and on the rocks," he said dryly as he handed it to her.

"Thank you." Lara almost wished he had forgotten.

His gaze strayed to the dance floor, picking out Trevor and Ann among the couples. Their steps matched well together, as naturally as a couple who had danced together many times before. There was a grimness about Rans's mouth as he glanced at the whiskey he held in his hand. Lara could only guess at the anger he must be feeling at the way Trevor was making a play for his girl.

"I'm sorry, but Trevor has a penchant for blondes," she stated, gazing at the pair, her eyes darkening to a troubled green.

"Jealous?" came his soft, husky voice.

"Yes." The answer was instinctive, voicing the truth that she was jealous of the blonde because she was Rans's date.

It was only after the admission had been made that Lara realized Rans meant jealous because

Ann was with Trevor. She could hardly correct her error so she let the answer stand.

As the music faded, the pair stopped dancing, yet didn't seem to be in any hurry to leave the floor as they talked and laughed. Another song began, a slower melody this time, and Rans turned to Lara.

"Shall we dance?" A challenging light glinted in his eyes.

Lara fought the impulse to accept wholeheartedly, glancing at her drink, intending to use it as an excuse not to have to endure the torture of being held in his arms. But his strong fingers closed around the glass and removed it from her hand, deliberately interpreting her silence as an acceptance.

"I—" Lara attempted a protest.

With the glasses set aside, his hand closed around hers and led her to the dance floor. Then Rans was pivoting her into his arms, a hand sliding around her waist.

"I guess I accept," she laughed, the sound brittle with tension.

"Did you want to wait there for them to come back?" Rans asked flatly.

Glancing to the edge of the dance floor, Lara saw Trevor eyeing her curiously. He knew she generally avoided dancing with anyone but older friends of her father's when they attended social functions. Her actions surprised him, but Trevor never let anything bother him too long. His dark head bent closer to the blond woman at his side. In the next moment they were returning to the floor.

"No, I didn't want to wait," Lara answered his question finally.

Her first few steps were awkward and uncoordinated as they began to dance to the slow music. She was trying desperately to control the desire to relax against Rans and let him lead her wherever he wanted to go. His physical attraction made such a desire too dangerous.

The stiffness of her limbs wasn't eased by the way he held her. His touch was hard and firm as though something inside him was tautly leashed. Lara stared at the knot of his tie, her heart hammering wildly in her throat. Peering through the top of her lashes, she studied the strong line of his jaw and moved her gaze upward. Hard brown eyes were looking beyond her, a savage glitter in their depths.

Hesitantly Lara glanced over her shoulder, finding the target of his look. Ann Koffman was molded against Trevor's length, her head resting against his shoulder as they moved sinuously to the slow tempo. Trevor's dark head was bent toward hers, smiling as he murmured near her ear.

Sharply averting her head from the scene, Lara met the rapier thrust of Rans's eyes. She paled under his piercing regard and looked swiftly away.

"Is this his usual practice when you go out?" A dry sarcasm laced his question.

"We rarely go out together," Lara corrected and paused nervously before answering. "If there is an attractive woman, Trevor usually pays attention to her. His ego can't tolerate it if a woman doesn't like him."

"Don't you do anything about it?"

"There isn't anything I can do." Or want to do, she could have added, but didn't.

"Isn't there?" He smiled crookedly, a wicked glint dancing roguishly in his eyes.

His forearm folded over hers, drawing her hand against the solid wall of his chest, her fingers clasped in the firm grip of his. The arm around her waist tightened to pull her closer until she was wrapped in a near embrace. Only a struggle would have freed her from his iron hold.

"Rans!" was her startled murmur of token resistance.

"Quiet," he ordered. "We are being observed so just listen to the music."

Out of the corner of her eye, Lara saw the frowning look Trevor was directing at them. Then the melody of the song captured her attention as she remembered a line from its lyrics. "My love, I've hungered for your touch a long, lonely time." With eyes closed, she surrendered to its truth and relaxed in Rans's strong arms.

It took all of her willpower to leave his arms when the song ended. Her ivory complexion was paler than normal, but her expression gave no indication of the withdrawal pains she suffered. It didn't falter under Trevor's scrutiny when they re-joined them.

Her father and Charlotte Thompson joined the four of them on the sidelines. Martin Alexander was in one of his garrulous moods, directing the conversation to his favorite topic—pecans. His presence in the group brought a continuous stream of guests stopping to chat for a minute or two before moving on to the dance floor or to the bar.

Rans had retrieved Lara's drink shortly after they had left the dance floor and had obtained one for Ann, who was now at his side. As much as she tried, Lara couldn't keep her attention focused on the conversation around her. She was too con-scious of Rans.

He was listening to her father, nodding now and then to some statement, yet he seemed very aloof as if a large part of his thoughts were elsewhere. His glass was refilled for the third time and Lara knew something was eating away at him. She could only guess that it had to do with Ann, whose gaze kept straying to Trevor.

A hand gripped her elbow and Lara glanced at its owner with a jerk of her head. Trevor smiled at her—the smug smile of a cat licking the cream from its whiskers.

"Let's dance," he said.

If she had expected him to ask anyone, it would have been the willowy blonde with Rans. The invi-tation had been issued loud enough for the others to hear. Under the circumstances Lara didn't see how she could refuse, so she let him escort her onto the dance floor.

Slipping an arm around her waist, Trevor murmured complacently, "You seem very interested in MacQuade tonight. Is there anything I should know?"

Her poise cracked only for an instant. "I haven't the slightest idea what you are talking about." An icy chill ran down her spine. If her preoccupation with Rans had been so obvious, perhaps others had noticed.

"Don't you?" he mocked. "I noticed you didn't object when he held you so closely while the two of you were dancing."

"Was there something wrong with that?" Lara remarked haughtily. "I don't believe the way we were dancing was much different from the way you and Miss Koffman were."

A dark brow arched in quizzical amusement. "Do I detect a note of jealousy in your tone? Maybe you aren't as indifferent to me as you like to pretend."

"You have a very vivid imagination, Trevor." She tipped her head back to glare at him with cold contempt.

"If it's not my attention you are trying to gain, then it must be MacQuade's," he pointed out with a speculative gleam in his dark eyes.

"Don't be absurd." But she had to look away.

"Why don't you be honest with yourself for

once, Lara?'' Trevor grinned mockingly. "I know MacQuade isn't your type, so why don't you simply admit that you are trying to make me jealous.''

Lara sincerely doubted that anyone could possess an ego as big as Trevor's. He was so absolutely positive that no woman would want another man if she could have him that Lara nearly laughed in his face. The only thing that stopped her was the sight of Rans guiding his date onto the floor.

"You are mistaken," she shrugged eloquently.

"I didn't realize you were so adept at playing games, Lara," he commented after considering a moment. "I'm willing to prolong the chase if that's what you want. It tends to heighten the thrill of capture.''

His hand slid suggestively downward from her hip. Her own hand quickly left his shoulder to check his caress. "Stop it," Lara warned beneath her breath.

And Trevor chuckled. "It's still too soon, is it?''

"It will always be too soon, " she stated acidly.

"Whatever you say," he smiled confidently. "I'm willing to play by your rules, with a few variations of my own.''

In the next few steps, his cryptic statement was explained when he paused alongside another couple. Lara's glance of vague curiosity encountered the sparkling blue lights of Ann's eyes. Suddenly wary, she looked back at Trevor. His dark gaze was directed at Rans.

"Shall we change partners?" Trevor suggested.

Lara sent up a silent prayer that Rans would refuse. He looked at her, the smoldering dark brown of his gaze almost curling her toes. Then it flicked arrogantly to Trevor.

"Permanently?" Rans questioned in a deceptively lazy tone.

Her heart leaped in spite of the common sense that told her it was only a joke. Trevor was momentarily disconcerted, too, but he recovered with a laugh.

"It's a thought, isn't it?" he replied in a humorous vein as he released Lara to Rans's waiting arms.

A tremor quivered through her at his firm touch. She had difficulty breathing when she felt the hardness of his thighs against her legs. Weakly she swayed closer until she felt his smoothly shaven jaw against her hair. His head jerked back as if she had burned him.

"I'm sorry," Lara mumbled self-consciously, stiffening her neck to move away.

"No." His voice was hard, denying her the right to move away. His head bent slightly to rest alongside her face.

"Please," she swallowed. His breath was warm against her cheek, smelling of alcohol. A strong thumb was absently rubbing the inside of her wrist. "I think you've had too much to drink," Lara breathed, feeling the heady intoxication of his body molded against hers.

"Enough it would seem," Rans chuckled lowly, drawing back to gaze into the disturbed greenness of her eyes, "to dare your claws in hopes of making you purr the way you once did."

"Don't," she protested.

"Don't you want to make your husband jealous?" he mocked.

Lara shook her head, needing to escape. "Let me go," she insisted shakily.

"The song isn't over yet," he reminded her complacently.

Blindly she stared at a button on his shirt. "Let me go," Lara repeated desperately.

There was an expressive shrug of his wide shoulders as his hold slackened. Unmindful of the curious looks, Lara walked unhurriedly from the dance floor, aware that Rans was following with leisurely strides. She knew he didn't intend to let her escape completely. She supposed that Rans was flirting with her to get revenge on Trevor for flirting with his date. And Lara didn't like being used that way, not when she was trying to control her own wayward emotions.

There was one place Rans couldn't follow and she slipped into the ladies' powder room. She took her time applying fresh lipstick and patting the smooth coiffure of her hair. When she peered out the door into the hall, there was no sign of Rans.

Cautiously she stepped out, avoiding the door leading into the private banquet room in favor of a rear exit door opening to the outside. The night was languidly still, a few crickets chirruping in the landscaped bushes. Lara stepped farther into the cool darkness, wrapping her arms around her middle in an attempt to ease the aching emptiness in her midsection. She silently wished for a cigarette to calm her jangled nerves, but had none in her small evening purse.

"Would you like a cigarette?"

At the sound of the familiarly husky voice, Lara jumped, pivoting sharply in alarm. A tall figure disassociated itself from the concealing shadows. Light from a three-quarter moon touched Rans MacQuade's face.

His rugged features were twisted in a cynical smile. "I've been waiting for you."

A cigarette burned in his hand as he placed a second between his lips and snapped a lighter flame to the end, handing it to Lara after an initial puff.

"I...I needed some fresh air," Lara faltered.

"That's what I thought," he responded dryly.

"Why are you here?"

"Because you are."

Lara turned away, unable to endure the lazy thoroughness of his gaze. "Why don't you leave me alone?" she murmured in despair. "Your Ann will be wondering where you are."

"And so will Trevor. Isn't that the whole point of this?" inquired Rans, moving forward into her line of sight and glancing casually skyward at the stars overhead.

"Trevor won't care," Lara replied tightly.

In fact, he would probably find the whole thing amusing. It would reinforce his opinion that Lara was attempting to make him jealous— which was preposterous and impossible since he felt no deep emotion for her—and it would give him a clear field with Ann Koffman.

"You have forgotten Trevor's ego." He studied the burning tip of his cigarette and the smoke curling in a gauzy gray ribbon from its tip.

"What do you mean?" she frowned, eyeing him uncomfortably.

"He isn't going to like it if he thinks his wife finds another man more attractive. If nothing else, curiosity will make him come after you."

"I don't particularly care." She stared stonily into the night, knowing that what Rans was really hoping was that Trevor would leave Ann alone.

"Don't you?" His cigarette was ground out beneath the heel of his shoe.

"No, I don't."

"You went along very willingly with the idea of making him jealous of you tonight," Rans pointed out. "You even admitted you were jealous when he was dancing with Ann. Is it pride that's making you say that you don't care?"

"I wasn't jealous!" Lara protested with irritation, and realized that she didn't want to explain that statement.

"Will you please go away and leave me alone?" she demanded.

"I swear half the time you don't know what you are saying or doing!" he muttered, his hand snaking out to seize her wrist. "You are a complete contradiction with your flaming hair and marble pale complexion." Lara twisted her arm, straining against his grip to no avail. "You swear you can't stand to be touched when the actual truth is just the opposite."

"Let me go, please." She was breathing quickly and unevenly, seeing the light in his eyes and knowing she didn't have the strength nor the desire to fight him off.

"No." He shook his sun-streaked head, a hand gripping her waist to draw her toward him. "We're going to see this thing through to the end."

His mouth closed over hers in hard possession, parting her unresisting lips for the exploration of his searching tongue. An explosion of fire raged through her veins. She didn't need the molding caress of his hands as she willingly arched her body against his solid outline, her fingers clutching the material of his jacket at the waves of weak submission that flowed through her muscles.

Lara's hungry response released a torrent of kisses that rained over her eyes and cheek and neck. Each one jolted her to her toes. She tried to return his passion and thrilled when she felt the trembling of his muscles. A large hand roughly cupped itself under the swelling curve of her breast as his mouth blazed a fiery trail to the shadowy cleft at the V neckline of her dress.

The outside door swished shut, bringing Lara partially to her senses, enough to realize that someone had seen them. Her hands pushed against his jacket.

"Rans, please," she begged for him to stop, while every fiber of her being pleaded with him to continue to not stop until they were both satisfied.

It was the latter that he listened to, laughing huskily as he nuzzled the side of her throat, nibbling sensuously at her earlobe until she moaned with the erotic mastery of his touch.

With the last ounce of her will, Lara protested sharply. "Stop." Rans started to ignore her again and she added, "You are drunk, Mr. MacQuade."

"Drunk?" Harsh laughter erupted from his throat as he drew his head back, his chest rising and falling in deep, disturbed breaths that didn't help Lara's emotions. "I am drunk. With liquor or with you, I don't know. They both burn and make me lose my head."

But he was in control of himself, Lara could see that in the piercing hardness of his eyes. His arms fell to his sides, leaving her skin cold where his touch had burned her minutes before. Inside she was crying, wanting him more than she had ever wanted him.

Everything had gone wrong. She hadn't wanted to come tonight. Now she regretted bitterly that she had. Instead of remembering Rans with another woman, the memory of what had happened this moment would be forever with her.

"Someone saw us," she breathed shakily.

"So?" Rans taunted. "Are you worried about your reputation?"

She turned abruptly away, his jeering words slashing at her heart, "No," she shook her head, her chin dipping downward in defeat.

"Don't worry," he mocked. "I doubt if it was anyone other than your husband. I know you'll excuse me now. Good evening, Mrs. Cochran."

Her chin was lifted and a hard kiss was branded on her mouth. Before her hands could touch him—to protest or deepen the kiss—he was gone, striding away toward the building. Lost and alone, Lara remained outside for several more minutes, wishing she didn't have to go in and face Rans again or argue with Trevor.

There wasn't any choice. Soon someone would come looking for her, more than likely Trevor if he had seen her locked in that embrace with Rans. She didn't want to see him alone yet, not until she had better control of herself.

Lara delayed rejoining the party by slipping into the powder room. Her eyes were red and swollen from unshed tears. While she was rinsing them with cold water, one of the dinner guests, Nora Evans, walked in.

"Oh, hello, Lara," she greeted with only mild surprise. "That smoke in the room really burns your eyes, doesn't it? It's almost a relief to get out of there."

"Yes, it is," Lara agreed, drying her eyes and reaching for her evening purse on the counter top. Quickly she reapplied her makeup, finishing as the woman was about to leave, and walked with her into the party room.

Trevor was at her side immediately, his dark eyes glittering with a knowing look leaving Lara with little doubt that he had seen her with Rans.

"There you are, darling." His arm circled her shoulders in seemingly affectionate possession. "I was beginning to worry about you."

The woman, old enough to be Trevor's mother, smiled with a trace of envy at the romantically handsome man and moved off in search of her balding husband. Lara remained rigidly erect against his touch.

His dark head bent to whisper mockingly in her ear. "MacQuade returned sometime ago. What took you so long?"

"That's none of your business," she murmured shortly.

He clicked his tongue in mock reproval. "You forget, my love, that I'm your husband."

Lara flashed him a cold look. "I try."

Black fires burned in his eyes at her rejection, his nostrils flaring in anger. Then, slowly, a cunning light entered his dark gaze.

"It was all part of your game, wasn't it?" Trevor smiled. "You surprise me Lara. I always thought you had too much moral pride. It seems I don't know you as well as I thought."

"You don't know me at all, Trevor. You never will. You are too egotistical and self-centered to bother about anyone but yourself," she retorted cuttingly. "Let's rejoin the others."

Trevor laughed softly and guided her toward the group dominated by her father. He was too arrogantly sure of his own attraction to believe there was any truth in her words, and he was making his own interpretations of her actions.

Covertly Lara searched the faces in the room. None belonged to Rans or Ann Koffman. Had they left? She longed to ask yet knew she didn't dare if she wanted to avoid more of Trevor's disgusting comments.

The pounding in her head that had been with her all evening in various degrees of discomfort began to increase. The steady chatter of voices, the loud music of the band and the smoke-filled room didn't help her headache. Overriding all of those was the tension.

A half an hour later, when Trevor suggested they leave, Lara could have cried with relief. She didn't even care why he wanted to leave the party so early. But Martin Alexander objected to their departure.

"Lara, you are the hostess. You can't leave," her father protested.

"I have a terrible headache, daddy. Besides," she cajoled desperately, "you are the guest of honor and your friends will be less inhibited if we youngsters leave."

"You do have a point there." His eyes twinkled merrily and Lara knew she had won.

She kissed him lightly on the cheek. "Happy Birthday, daddy," she murmured. "And give our goodbyes to the others."

Minutes later she was relaxing against the plush upholstery of Trevor's Seville. Closing her eyes, she listened to the silence, the powerful motor sounding as only a contented purr inside the car. Pine trees crowded the sides of the road, serrated silhouettes against a moonlit sky.

The car made a turn and slowed to a stop. Lara opened her eyes, expecting to see the lighted entrance of her home. There wasn't a building in sight, only the forests and the tan ribbon of the dirt road. Her gaze swung warily to Trevor. He was sitting sideways in his seat, quietly watching her.

"Why have we stopped here?" Lara was instantly on guard.

His hand moved toward the dashboard of the car. There was a click, then soft music caressed the night. Trevor took his time in answering.

"Do you remember when we were dating?" he mused. From the shadowy darkness of his side of the car, Lara could feel his gaze roaming over her smooth features. "We used to park along some isolated stretch of the road, listen to music and talk . . . and kiss."

"I remember." Wondering how she could have been so naive to believe all the lies and romantic compliments he had made then. "It was all very long ago, Trevor." There was a hint of acid distaste for the subject in her tone as she leaned her head against the raised seat back. "Please take me home now."

Not a sound betrayed his movement. The spicy scent of his cologne warned Lara of his nearness an instant before his lips pressed against hers. Repulsed, she twisted her mouth away, her hands raising to push against his chest.

"Stop it!" she snapped angrily, hunching her shoulder against his attempt to bury his mouth along her neck. "I'm not in the mood for a wrestling match with you. I have a headache and I want to go home!"

Trevor simply laughed, pressing her back against the seat with his weight. "That's a very unoriginal excuse, my adoring wife."

Sickeningly, Lara realized that he was not going to be put off with mere words. He had seen the way she had responded to Rans and intended to penetrate her glacial coldness. She fought his mouth and roving hands that left her feeling dirty and unclean. The more she struggled, the more excited he seemed to become.

The nightmare grew to terrifying proportions as Lara felt the fragile material of her dress ripping at the shoulder. The moistness of his mouth nibbled at her bared skin, sending shudders of revulsion down her spine. She freed an arm from the pinning weight of his chest and raked her fingernails across his face.

With a yelping curse, Trevor moved away, a hand instinctively cupping his wounded cheek. He held it away, staring at the traces of smeared blood in the palm with disbelief. A black rage distorted his handsome features.

Lara didn't wait for the explosion. With wrenching sobs of panic, she pushed open the door, her legs quivering with fear. Trevor reached for her, his fingers closing over the skirt of her dress. She tore it away, uncaring of the second rip that ruined the expensive dress.

"Come back here!" Trevor snarled, moving across the seat to follow her.

She tried to slam the door in his face, but his arm reached out to stop it. Wildly she glanced around for help, but the road was completely deserted.

Trevor was stepping out of the car, the moonlight illuminating the claw marks disfiguring his cheek. "I'll get even with you for this," he threatened. "Now get back in the car."

There was a brief, negative shake of her head, then Lara bolted, running down the road. She could hear the crunch of gravel behind her and realized Trevor was chasing her. The high heels of her shoes slowed her down. It was only a matter of seconds before he caught up with her.

Turning abruptly, she stumbled down the ditch

alongside the road and raced into the pinewoods. The towering trunks closed around her protectively, hiding her within seconds from his sight. She was making too much noise of her own to tell if he was still following her, but Lara could hear him angrily yelling her name. It made her run faster.

CHAPTER NINE

AHEAD, A LIGHT SHONE through the trees. Winded and sobbing between gulps for air, Lara staggered toward it, her heels sinking in the soft mulch of pine needles. She had no idea where she was or which direction to go to reach her home, but the light promised safety.

As she drew nearer, a small house took shape, standing alone in a thin stand of pines. A dirt road stretched in front of it. The light she had seen gleaming through a window beckoned her toward the porch.

Out of the darkness, a hand grabbed her, then a second. A gasping scream ripped from her throat. Lara struggled wildly like a frightened animal trapped in a snare, but the iron hands easily overcame her attempt, giving her a hard shake that rattled her teeth.

"Lara, stop it!" a voice commanded harshly.

Her gaze focused on the bronzed features of Rans MacQuade and she collapsed weakly against him, winding her arms around his neck and sobbing her relief into his shirt.

"Rans, help me." The breathless plea released a torrent of tears.

The hands at her waist denied her the support of his body, holding her away from him. His piercing gaze swept over her in rapid inspection noting the torn material at the shoulder of her dress.

"What happened?" Rans snapped.

"Oh, please," Lara swayed toward him and he gathered her against his chest. "You've got to help me," she sobbed as his hand gently smoothed the hair away from her face. "He—he—" Convulsive shudders wracked her body, making her words incoherent jibberish.

"Who?" His fingers closed punishingly around her throat, tilting her head back. "Who did this to you?" he demanded savagely.

At first Lara could only shake her head mutely, not wanting to talk. She only wanted to be held in his arms and feel his warmth while she tried to forget the horrible memory of Trevor's repulsive touch.

"Answer me!" Rans glowered, giving her another hard shake. "Who did this?"

Her trembling lips finally moved. "Tr-Trevor," she answered through her choking sobs. "He ... he tried to m-make love to m-me I ... I—" Lara shuddered uncontrollably again.

Violently Rans thrust her away from him, scornful contempt carved in his rugged features. "That's what you wanted, wasn't it?" he jeered.

"You wanted to make him jealous and take notice of you."

"No." Her head moved disbelievingly to the side.

"Come on, Mrs. Cochran. I was there," he laughed harshly.

"I never wanted him to touch me," Lara breathed, tears drenching her face.

"He's your husband. He has a right to his connubial pleasures."

"No." Closing her eyes, she surrendered to the tremors of revulsion that quaked through her. "He makes me feel...dirty." Salty tears blurred her vision when she tried to look at Rans. "No one...no one understands. No one."

Tiredness engulfed, the tiredness of defeat. It was no good explaining. Rans wasn't listening to her. Nothing she said made the slightest impression. Blindly she turned away, silent sobs of wretched misery shaking her shoulders.

Behind her, Rans swore softly, then his hands were turning her into his arms. Lara resisted briefly then buried her head in the inviting expanse of his chest and wept. His hand stroked her hair in a soothing caress.

Finally there were only hiccuping sobs left. She had cried out all her pain and torment and degradation until she felt hollow and completely empty inside. She was numb to any emotion.

Wearily Lara lifted her head from his chest. A crisp white handkerchief touched her cheek, wiping the dampness from her skin. She glanced up gratefully to see a faint smile of gentleness touching the corners of his mouth.

"Your mascara is running all over the place," Rans murmured.

He stood silently, inches from her as she took the handkerchief and scrubbed her face. A few minutes later she handed it back, her breathing still shaky and uneven.

"Come on." His hand closed firmly on her elbow. "I'll drive you home."

The pickup truck was parked on the opposite side of the house. In the cab, Lara leaned weakly against the seat, too tired to care where she was going or what might be waiting for her when she reached her destination. Rans was sitting beside her and temporarily at least, she felt safe.

When the truck stopped in the cul de sac drive, Lara stared woodenly at the light streaming from the long windows flanking the front door. Her door was opened and Rans reached forward to help her out. She fumbled through her purse for the door key and placed it in his hand. It was several seconds before his fingers closed around it in acceptance.

Once the door was unlocked, he followed her into the entry hall, glancing around the silent house. There was no sign or sound of anyone else in the house. Returning the key, Rans studied the dispirited lines etched in her pale features.

"You're tired," he said quietly. "Sleep will help you forget what happened."

Instantly an image of Trevor flashed in her mind's eye. The murderous rage that had been in his expression sent a shiver down her spine. Her widened green eyes swung to the staircase. Was he upstairs waiting for her? The thought chilled her to the bone. Mutely Lara appealed to Rans, like a child wanting the last of its fears to be laid to rest.

An impatient sigh broke from the grim line of his mouth. "Come on."

A guiding hand rested lightly on the small of her back as he turned her toward the stairs. Their footsteps echoed hollowly through the empty house.

Without a word, Rans checked her room and the locked adjoining door to Trevor's room. There was no one upstairs, either. Lara hovered near the foot of her bed, feeling awkward and foolish. Her gaze skittered away when he glanced at her.

"I don't think you have anything to worry about. Your father will probably be home shortly," he said.

"Yes," she agreed with a self-conscious nod. He walked to the door. "Thank you," Lara offered hesitantly. Rans nodded curtly, stepping into the second-floor hallway and closing her bedroom door.

For several seconds she listened to his departing footsteps. Her throat ached as she walked to the closet for her nightgown. Sighing, she realized that Rans was right and there wasn't anything more to worry about.

Trevor wouldn't bother her. He probably would not even come home tonight if he reverted to his usual custom that had followed their previous, bitterly angry arguments. No doubt his injured pride would seek solace in some other woman's arms tonight.

Slowly Lara undressed and slipped on the mint-green nightgown, the lightweight material falling loosely around her ankles. Sitting in front of the vanity mirror, she began to brush her hair, prolonging the moment when she had to crawl into the empty bed. She was tired, wearily so, but she was afraid that once in bed she would start thinking.

There were only two things to think about, and she didn't want to face the truth of either of them. She didn't want to admit there was anything to face. Neither could she spend the rest of the night brushing her hair.

Resolutely, Lara set the brush down and walked to the table lamp at her bedside, twisting the knob on. As she turned to walk to the overhead light switch on the wall, her bedroom door was opened. Lara halted in surprise when Rans stood in the opening.

Behind her, the light from the bedside lamp made the thin fabric of her nightgown appear transparent, revealing the nakedness it was meant to conceal. Tension gripped both of them, electric and sensual.

"I thought you had gone," Lara whispered at last. Her pulse skipped rapidly with joy that he had not.

"I—" Rans breathed in deeply, seeming to gather his control. His gaze swerved to the cup in his hand, its expression hard and impassive when it returned to her. "I took the liberty of fixing you some cocoa. You looked in need of something to relax you."

Abruptly he set the cup and saucer on the dresser near the door and turned as if to leave. Lara stepped quickly forward, desperately wanting him to stay.

"Don't go!" she called to him, and hesitated when he pivoted sharply toward her, the chiseled lines of his face drawn into a forbidding mask. "Can't you stay and...and talk to me? I don't want to be alone."

"Talk?" His short laugh was harsh. His gaze raked her insolently. "With you dressed like that, do you think if I stayed we would talk? My God, what do you think I am?"

Her hands crossed defensively over the bodice of her gown. Lara reached quickly for the robe lying across the bed, holding it in front of her, but not putting it on.

"I don't want you to leave," she protested weakly.

A smile, cold with amusement, cynically twisted his mouth. "Good night, Mrs. Cochran." His sardonic voice underlined the marital term of address.

"Don't call me that!" she flared.

Lara crossed the room on wings of hurt anger

only to have it fade to nothing when she reached him. Her green eyes searched his impassive face for some sign that would give her hope. Her chin quivered at his unrelenting hardness.

"Don't you want to stay?" Lara's whispered plea throbbed with the aching need she felt.

His fingers bit savagely into her shoulders, while a muscle twitched uncontrollably along his jaw. Languidly, Lara melted against his body, masculine and strong.

"Do you think I don't want to stay?" The smoldering light of desire glittered in his brown eyes. Her heart rocketed at the sight of it as his gaze swept possessively over her face and the lacy neckline of her nightgown. "Damn, but you're a witch, Lara," Rans muttered thickly. "I—"

Her fingertips touched his lips, checking their flow of words. She felt all feminine and enticing, no longer struggling against the waywardness of her emotions.

"You said my name," she murmured. "You used it earlier tonight, but I was too frightened and I wanted to hear you say it again ... Rans." Lovingly she let his name roll from her tongue.

He turned his head away, breaking free from the touch of her fingertips. "You are making it impossible," Rans breathed heavily.

"Why?" Lara smiled, knowing she was disturbing him as he had disturbed her so often.

"I have only one rule as far as women are concerned," he said flatly. "I stay away from the ones

who are married. And like it or not, Mrs. Cochran—" his voice lashed silently as his hands firmly
pushed her away from him "—you are married."

"Rans." Pain choked off the rest of her protest.
Instead she asked breathlessly, "If I wasn't married?"

An eyebrow slashed upward with arrogant cyni-
cism. "Is there any likelihood of that?" Rans
taunted. Lara hesitated, unable to answer him immediately. "That's what I thought. Good night,
Mrs. Cochran."

"Rans, no!" she called out to him as he spun
away to stride into the hall.

His step didn't slacken as if he was determined
to get as far away from her as possible in the short-
est amount of time. On shaking legs, Lara followed him. She reached the top of the stairs as he
opened the front door on the ground floor.

"Rans, wait." The door was slammed shut. "I
love you." The admission was out in the open,
her voice trailing forlornly into a whisper when
Lara realized she was the only one who had heard
it.

The pickup truck roared out of the driveway.
Slowly Lara retraced her steps to the bedroom, ignoring the cup of cocoa on her dresser to curl into
a tight ball of pain and misery beneath the covers
of her bed.

The next morning Lara slept late, mentally and
physically exhausted from the turmoil. She had
just dressed and was walking toward the stairs

when she heard voices in the hall below. One was her father's and the second belonged to Rans. Lara hurried to catch him, wanting to speak to him even if it was too soon, but the front door was closing as she reached the landing.

"Was that Rans?" she questioned her father, taking the last few steps with skipping feet. "Is he leaving?"

A puzzled frown creased his forehead when he turned to her. "How did you know?"

"I heard his voice. I have to talk to him." Lara raced toward the door in time to see the rear of the pickup driving down the lane. "Did he say where he was going?"

"No." Martin Alexander shook his head, running his fingers through the sides of salted auburn hair. "Where's Trevor? I've got to talk to him about this." Lara noticed the paper her father had clutched in his hand. "I imagine if Rans told you, he told Trevor, too. I just don't understand," he sighed.

"What?" His sentences were confusing her. "What was Rans supposed to have told me?" Was her father referring to last night? She didn't understand.

"About him leaving, of course," he answered impatiently. "Did he explain his reasons to you?"

"Leaving," Lara breathed, her face growing pale.

"Yes, leaving!" Her father waved the paper in

the air. "He even put his resignation in writing. A two-week notice and the name of a man qualified to replace him."

"Why?" In her heart she guessed the reason.

"That's what I'm asking you!" he retorted. "You were the one who said you knew he was leaving."

"No, I...I only meant was he leaving the house. I had no idea at all that he had quit," Lara explained. "What...what reason did he give for leaving?"

"Oh, some mumbo-jumbo about the job not turning out to be the kind of thing he wanted," her father shrugged absently, his brow furrowed in concentration.

"Surely you tried to talk him out of it?"

"Of course," he sighed, and rubbed his forehead. "I offered him more money, a part ownership in the farm, a new house, a new car. I tried everything, but he kept insisting that he was still dissatisfied and nothing would change that. I nearly got down on my hands and knees and begged him to stay. I couldn't have found a better man for the job than Rans if I had ordered him directly from heaven. And now what?" He lifted his hands in a helpless gesture.

"He can't leave," Lara whispered. Her father was too concerned with his own problem to hear the pulsing ache in her soft voice.

"Maybe Trevor can talk him out of it, or at least we can put our heads together and come up with some kind of a plan. Where is he?" Martin glanced toward the stairs. "Is he still in bed?"

"He didn't come home last night," she answered swallowing back the lump in her throat.

"Didn't come home? You two left the party together last night? How could he bring you home and not come home himself?" he demanded incredulously. "Where is he?"

"I don't know and I don't care!" The details of last night would require too much telling for Lara to want to spend the time explaining. "It doesn't matter what you think anymore, daddy. I'm divorcing Trevor as quickly as I can see an attorney and get the legal papers filed. Our marriage has been dead for a long while. It's time it was buried. So Trevor isn't going to be much help to you whenever he does come back. And you can tell him what I said, if I'm not here."

"What are you talking about? What's going on?" His confusion increased as Lara opened the front door. "Where are you going?"

"To talk to Rans."

"Well, see if you can talk him into staying!" he called after her. "Rans might be at the cattle barns."

Racing around the side of the house, Lara realized that now that she had faced the truth, it really hadn't been such a difficult thing. What would hurt was if she had left it too late. Her fear now was that Rans would really leave.

Behind the wheel of her blue Mustang, she

stepped on the accelerator, the tires churning up a cloud of dust as they tried to answer the demand for speed. The pace didn't slacken until she reached the breeding pens two miles from the main house. The rust-colored head of a Santa Gertrudis bull lifted curiously when she turned into the lane to the barns.

Rans's pickup truck was parked beneath a large oak. Lara stopped her car beside it, stepping out before the engine died. At first glance there was no sign of activity in any of the barns. Despairing, Lara thought she would have to search each of the large structures, then there was movement near one of the large double doors.

She held her breath, letting it out slowly when Rans appeared. Sunlight glinted on the amber highlights in his brown hair. The white of his shirt contrasted sharply with the dark tan of his sun-browned features, chiseled into an expressionless mask. Snug-fitting Levis of faded blue molded the muscular length of his legs, striding purposefully forward.

There was a slight narrowing of his gaze as he saw Lara poised beside her car. His stride faltered for an instant, then continued in a direct line toward his truck. Lara realized he had no intention of speaking to her and she walked swiftly to intercept him.

"Rans, please, I want to talk to you," she explained hurriedly as he drew near her.

His glance, dispassionate and aloof, swept over

her briefly. "We don't have anything to discuss, Mrs. Cochran," with deliberate emphasis on her name.

"Yes, we do," Lara protested. "You can't leave, Rans, not now."

"I see your father told you I was quitting," he interrupted briskly, not slackening his long stride to match her smaller steps.

"Yes. Rans, I have to know why, please."

"I gave him my reason. I'll let it stand." He opened the door of his pickup and would have crawled in if Lara hadn't caught at his arm to stop him. He looked down at her coldly.

"You have to listen to me. I wanted to explain to you last night, but you left before I had a chance," Lara declared earnestly.

"I've heard it all before," Rans replied disinterestedly. "As far as I'm concerned, last night never happened. I've handed in my resignation, and there is nothing you can say that will change my mind. Do I need to make it any plainer than that?"

Recoiling a step as if he had struck her, she stared at him, unable to believe the rejection his words implied. When her hand fell away from his arm, he stepped into the cab of the truck, started the motor and drove away without another glance at Lara as she stood in stunned silence.

The truck had disappeared on the graveled road before she moved, walking numbly to her own car. Her hands clasped the steering wheel and Lara bowed her head against them, intense pain sweeping through her. She didn't want to believe what she had heard.

He had not even listened to her, nor allowed her the opportunity to explain. The only sentence that gave her any hope at all was his comment that he had heard it all before.

It was a hope as slim as a wishbone, but it was the only one she had. She needed it. The next few days would not be easy. Lifting her head, Lara smiled tightly. First things first, she told herself, turning the key in the ignition.

But if Rans MacQuade thought he had heard the last from her, he was very much mistaken. Alexanders did not give up very easily, as he would soon discover. She shifted the car into gear, driving at a much slower rate back to the main house, using the time to think of how she was going to deal with her father and Trevor. Again the thought returned that the next few days would not be easy, but nothing that was ultimately worthwhile was easy.

CHAPTER TEN

LARA NIBBLED AT HER FINGERNAIL. Her anxious gaze swung from the sun-bathed courtyard to her father, who was seated behind the mahogany desk. A black telephone receiver was in one hand while the other tapped the eraser end of a pencil on the table.

"You see that he gets the message immediately, Tom," Martin Alexander instructed into the phone, then replaced it in its cradle.

"Well?" Lara prompted. "Is he coming?"

"I don't see how he can possibly avoid it," he answered with a smiling shake of his head.

Suppressing a shiver, Lara turned back to the courtyard scene. "What are we going to do if this doesn't work, daddy?" she murmured.

"We will think of something." The chair squeaked. A few seconds later she felt his hands curving around the soft flesh of her upper arms. "I'm sorry, pet. I don't know if I've got around to saying that yet or not. I wasn't a very understanding father."

"You meant well." Lara turned her head, glancing up to the concerned brown eyes. "I just didn't tell you everything, that's all." She smiled reassuringly. "Let's face it, daddy, we are both Alexanders, and sometimes we have to be hit in the face with the truth before we'll accept it.

"A sheer case of too damned much pride." He winked and lightly kissed her cheek. "If we don't want our plan to fall apart, I'd better leave. It's not going to take Rans long to get here from the sheds once Tom delivers the message."

If he comes, Lara thought silently. In the last ten days, Rans had avoided her and the house like the plague. Every attempt she had made to speak to him had been met with defeat. But Martin Alexander was still his employer for a few more days, and he could hardly ignore a direct order—she hoped.

"I'll be back in, oh, about two hours." Her father moved away toward the hall door. "Good luck, pet."

"Daddy?" Lara turned, her voice checking his departure at the door. "Thanks...for all you're doing."

A rueful smile curved his mouth. "After the callous advice I gave you the last time you came to me, this is the least I can do."

With a wave of his hand, he was out the door. Several minutes later, Lara heard the sound of his car pulling out of the drive. The clock ticked loudly in the silent house, the hands on the dial moving much too slowly.

Restlessly she walked from the study to the living room, counting the ticking seconds as she twisted her hands nervously, her left hand bare of any rings. She hovered beside a window looking out onto the front lawn.

Her heart stopped when a pickup truck turned into the driveway. The plan had worked thus far. Stifling the impulse to race to the front door, Lara waited at the window, well back so she couldn't be observed from the outside.

Rans swung his long frame out of the truck, hesitated as he glanced at the house, then slammed the cab door. There was an impatient spring to his stride and his mouth had thinned to a forbidding line. Inhaling deeply, Lara didn't move until she heard the knock at the door.

Her palms were moist with nervous perspiration. She dried them self-consciously in a smoothing gesture down the sides of her green plaid slacks. Her pulse was throbbing erratically and her legs were weak as they carried her to the front door.

Rans looked at her as she opened the door, his expression granite-hard. "Your father left a message that it was imperative he see me at once," he said tersely, without even offering a polite greeting.

Lara swallowed, unable to smile even stiffly. With a nod of her head, she stepped away from the door, holding it open untl he had walked into the hall. Rans didn't stop, but continued toward the study, ignoring her existence completely.

Her heart was in her throat as she followed him. A step inside the empty room, he pivoted. His gaze flicked to her whip sharp. The blood mounted in her face at his accusing look.

"He's not here," she explained unnecessarily. "He had to leave unexpectedly."

A dark eyebrow shot up in sardonic disbelief, freezing scorn in the glitter of his brown eyes. "I'll come back when he's here."

"No, wait," Lara hurried, trying to remain calm but unnerved by his uncompromising hardness. "He asked me to give you a message."

"Very well." Rans moved to one side as Lara entered the room, his mouth thinning into a grim line.

His alert gaze watched her walk to the desk and pick up the folded paper lying to the front. Her shaking fingers held it for an instant as she sent up a silent prayer, then turned, holding it out for Rans to take. His hand reached forward, but stopped short of the paper when he recognized it.

"You have the wrong paper." His hand fell back to his side. "That is my letter of resignation."

"Yes, I know." Lara's voice quivered in spite of her efforts. "My father wants you to reconsider it."

"No." Rans turned abruptly, terminating the conversation with his action.

"Not to stay on permanently," Lara rushed, "but just for a few more weeks. That's all he's asking. Things are in somewhat of a turmoil around here. I don't know if you've heard."

Rans paused near the door, but kept his back to her. "Martin has my notice. If my leaving has put things in a turmoil, then it is his problem. I made my recommendation for a replacement and would have been able to work with him this past week if your father had hired him, or anyone else. Since he didn't see fit to do it, I don't see any reason to stay any longer than my two weeks."

"He's been busy trying to find someone to take over Trevor's work." Lara held her breath as Rans hesitated again, letting it out slowly in relief when he turned. "You haven't heard?" she breathed.

His gaze sliced over her. "I've been too busy to listen to gossip. What happened?" he taunted coldly. "Was he sued for breach of promise by one of his mistresses? The scandal would be quite a blow to your self-righteous pride, wouldn't it? He was supposed to keep his affairs discreet."

His words were meant to hurt, and Lara winced at the pain they inflicted. "I've filed for divorce. Trevor has left."

She had been afraid that Rans had known and that it hadn't made any difference to his decision. But the flicker of surprise in his expression dismissed that possibility.

"Since when?" He clipped out the question.

"Since a week ago Sunday." Lara waited. When he didn't respond, but kept studying her with narrowed look, she continued anxiously. "With both you and Trevor leaving within days of each other, it puts a heavy burden on my father. Would you consider staying on . . . for a while longer?"

A frown creased his forehead as Rans breathed in deeply and walked to the courtyard doors. "Is Trevor's absence supposed to make a difference to me?"

Nervously, she clasped the paper in both hands, "I hoped it would." She stared at it, the words blurring in front of her eyes.

Glancing over his shoulder, he impaled her on his thrusting gaze. "Why?"

Widened eyes, shimmering and green, met his without flinching. "Because I want you to stay."

"Because of your father?" Rans persisted, not lessening the intensity of his piercing gaze.

There was a tenseness about him. He seemed to be holding himself rigidly still as if his tall, muscular frame was carved from stone. Lara kept wondering if she was battering her head uselessly against a rock wall that nothing she said would penetrate.

"Partly," she acknowledged, dipping her chin. "He needs you."

"What's the other part?"

Achingly Lara's gaze studied his face, the roughly hewn jaw and chin, the faint lines around his eyes that crinkled when he smiled and the dimpling clefts in his cheeks, the firm line of his mouth, the wide tanned forehead framed by thick, tobacco-brown hair. He was so aggressively virile that her whole body throbbed with his nearness.

"Don't you know?" she whispered.

"No."

A heavy silence weighted the room while Rans waited for her answer. Lara gathered what little of her pride that remained and threw it away.

"Because I'm in love with you, Rans." Her voice quivered. "In my heart I divorced Trevor a long time ago."

Slowly he crossed the room, not releasing her from his pinning gaze. His hands settled on her shoulders, their touch making her sway toward him, but he firmly kept her away.

"Are you sure?" His fingers dug into her flesh as if he meant to shake the truth out of her.

"Very sure," she smiled tremulously.

Some of the hardness began to leave his expression as if the rock wall had started to crumble. "Am I a fool to believe you?" he mused absently, his gaze traveling over the cascading red gold curls falling loosely around her shoulders and returning to the jewel brightness of her eyes.

"Probably," Lara murmured. "I'm headstrong and independent and spoiled. I lose my temper at the drop of a hat. And I'll probably turn into a jealous shrew when I'm old and wrinkled and not pretty enough anymore to make you—"

His mouth closed over hers in a bruising kiss to stop the enumeration of her faults. She melted against him, deepening the kiss with the hungry response of her own lips. Roughly his hands pulled her nearer. The torrid embrace stretched into minutes until Rans gained control of the fire raging inside. Lara's arms remained locked around him as she nestled her head against his chest, the pounding of his heart sounding joyfully in her ears.

"You will stay. Promise me you will never leave." She tipped her head back to gaze at him.

"You will play hell getting rid of me, wildcat," Rans growled affectionately, his fingers twisting into the flame gold of her long hair.

The light radiating from the velvet brown of his eyes took her breath away, at once possessive and passionate and gentle. A sensation of buoyancy seemed to fill her as if she was floating on a cloud.

"Tell me why, Rans?" whispered Lara, watching the hard lips and waiting for them to form the three precious words she was aching to hear.

He didn't disappoint her. "I love you that's why." The iron band of his embracing arms tightened like a vise, crushing her against his trembling length. He pressed his mouth against her temple, murmuring against her skin, "I love you, Lara. I love you." Repeating it as if the words had been bottled up too long inside of him.

Her fingers spread, moving over his back and shoulders in an exploring caress. "I love you too, darling." She rubbed her head against his chin and mouth, dissolving with a completeness of her emotion.

A tenseness seemed to take possession of him. "The way you loved Trevor?"

"Oh, no," Lara denied with a smiling sigh. "I loved his image. I was in love with love. His touch never shattered. His kiss never destroyed. I never felt alive, every nerve tingling, with him the way I do with you. There was always something missing that made me feel incomplete. But not anymore, not when you hold me. It's as if I've come home at last."

"To stay, Lara," he declared firmly, "because I'll never let you go."

"I'll die if you do." She shuddered, remembering the desolation that nearly entered her life when she had thought she might never see him again. "You quit because of me, didn't you?" she breathed.

"Why else?" His mouth crooked into a dry smile as he drew his head back to let his gaze rove possessively over her upturned face. "The job, the work, was everything I ever wanted. I knew that within a few weeks after I arrived. What I hadn't counted on was a beautiful redhead complicating the situation. I managed to ignore you quite successfully for a while. But you kept getting under my skin." Rans chuckled softly, his hands lightly caressing her feminine curves. "I thought you were a frigid piece of baggage, a stunningly wrapped block of ice. It was a challenge to keep chipping away to see if it was solid."

Lara leaned back against his arms, her hands

sliding to his broad chest. An impish light gleamed in her green eyes as she met the glittering fire of his gaze.

"My first impression of you was that you were arrogant." Her lips trying to conceal the smile hovering at the corners. "And I haven't revised my opinion at all."

The dimples came into play, carving bewitching clefts in his tanned cheeks while his eyes crinkled at the corners. "You should have," Rans told her, "because with you I was never certain about anything except how much I wanted you. The night I walked home from the stable was possibly the longest walk I ever took. I had found the volcano under the ice cap and I had to come to grips with the way I was really feeling toward you."

"That night was a revelation to me, too," Lara admitted. "I had thought I was immune to any physical need. Before I was revolted by a man's touch. But not that night. You wiped out the illusion that I was somehow different from everyone else. It was a frightening discovery."

"How do you think I felt, realizing I was falling in love with another man's wife?" A muscle twitched in his jaw. Lara caressed it tenderly to ease his remembered pain. "I had to keep reminding myself you were married and didn't belong to me. And you didn't make things any easier," Rans accused with mocking gruffness.

"I couldn't help it. I wanted you, too," she defended herself.

"I know. That's why I was leaving." He smiled fleetingly. "I knew that if I stayed, it was only a matter of time and I'd have you. I also knew I could never be satisfied with merely possessing you. I wanted you for my wife, to live with me, bear my name and my children. The prospect of an affair filled me with a bitterness that would eventually have destroyed both of us." His mouth closed briefly over hers in a hard kiss. "And that is my proposal of marriage, darling. Do you accept?"

"Yes." Lara breathed the answer that had been written in her face since Rans had taken her in his arms.

His hold tightened punishingly around her. An almost inaudible groan came from his throat as he crushed her against him. "How in the world are we going to make it until your divorce is final?" he muttered into the fiery silk of her hair.

"I can survive anything as long as you love me," was her whispered reply.

"Maybe you can fly to Reno or Mexico," Rans suggested thickly while her fingers lovingly explored the rugged contours of his face. "I don't want to wait another day."

"Neither do I. We'll find a way, darling, and we'll find it together," Lara promised.

"We'll start a new tradition." There was a wicked glint in his eyes as a roguish smile spread across his face. "The MacQuade brides always live happily ever after."

my VALENTINE 1992

Celebrate the most romantic day of the year with
MY VALENTINE 1992—a sexy new collection of four
romantic stories written by our famous Temptation
authors:

> GINA WILKINS
> KRISTINE ROLOFSON
> JOANN ROSS
> VICKI LEWIS THOMPSON

My Valentine 1992—an exquisite escape into a romantic
and sensuous world.

 Harlequin Books ®

VAL-92-R

HARLEQUIN *Temptation*

Rebels & Rogues

All men are not created equal. Some are rough around the edges. Tough-minded but tenderhearted. Incredibly sexy. The tempting fulfillment of every woman's fantasy.

When it's time to fight for what they believe in, to win that special woman, our Rebels and Rogues are heroes at heart.

Matt: A hard man to forget... and an even harder man not to love.

THE HOOD by *Carin Rafferty*.
Temptation #381, February 1992.

Cameron: He came on a mission from light-years away... then a flesh-and-blood female changed everything.

THE OUTSIDER by *Barbara Delinsky*.
Temptation #385, March 1992.

At Temptation, 1992 is the Year of Rebels and Rogues. Look for twelve exciting stories, one each month, about bold and courageous men.

Don't miss upcoming books by your favorite authors, including Candace Schuler, JoAnn Ross and Janice Kaiser.

RR-2